Patchwork Dolls

PATCHWORK DOLLS

stories

YSABELLE CHEUNG

— BLAIR —

Printed in the United States of America
Cover design by Laura Williams
Interior design by April Leidig

Blair is an imprint of Carolina Wren Press.

The mission of Blair/Carolina Wren Press is to seek out, nurture, and promote literary work by new and underrepresented writers.

We gratefully acknowledge the ongoing support of general operations by the Durham Arts Council's United Arts Fund and the North Carolina Arts Council.

The stories in this collection are works of fiction. As in all fiction, the literary perceptions and insights are based on experience; however, all names, characters, places, and incidents are either products of the author's imagination or are used fictitiously. No reference to any real person is intended or should be inferred.

Library of Congress Cataloging-in-Publication Data
Names: Cheung, Ysabelle, 1989– author
Title: Patchwork dolls / Ysabelle Cheung.
Other titles: Patchwork dolls (Compilation)
Description: Durham : Blair, 2026.
Identifiers: LCCN 2025025306 (print) | LCCN 2025025307 (ebook) |
ISBN 9781958888643 paperback | ISBN 9781958888711 ebook
Subjects: LCGFT: Fiction | Short stories
Classification: LCC PR9450.9.C54 P38 2026 (print) | LCC PR9450.9.C54 (ebook)
LC record available at https://lccn.loc.gov/2025025306
LC ebook record available at https://lccn.loc.gov/2025025307

Contents

Patchwork Dolls

Mycomorphosis

The morning of the fall, Noel was followed by a filmy, vegetal smell—dreams that she was being buried in cold soil. Then her phone grunted angrily. Two messages from her mother, three missed calls from her employer. She was late.

In a fluorescent-tinted coffee shop, her employer, a China studies professor, sternly told her that she was late on various assignments. When he gestured, she tried not to flinch but instead sucked in more air, coffee-bitter and moist.

On the subway ride back to her apartment, she noticed the train cars were slick with dirt; she saw it on everybody's skin, that same burnished layer of fermenting heat and oil. A man muttered to himself in the corner seat as she edged her way inside. *You, you, you,* the man said. *You, I'm going to get you. Oh, I'm going to get you. Yes, I'm going to get you.*

An MTA worker announced overhead that they would be stuck in the tunnel until further notice. She tried not to touch anything and silently pushed down an incoming panic attack.

Back at the apartment, she drew a bath to calm her nerves. It had been humid all day, so wet that the towels slid to the floor. Outside, a truck was backing up, and a new store had installed speakers that hosed the streets with noise. Car alarms screamed.

Her upstairs neighbors bickered over their small child. She felt like a sieve through which these sounds entered and left, leaving specks of anxious pollutants each time. Washing herself, she listed all the things she had to do. Ask her landlord to fix the gas. Request an extension on rent. Index her employer's paper. Pay monthly federal student loans. Message her mother back. Toss leftover food in the fridge. File taxes. Review insurance claim forms again.

She looked at herself in the mirror near the bathtub, the heated silvers of water knives on her skin. From ear to nose she tracked the scar that lay across her face, like a shriveled wad of paper mapping her cheek. In the subway, it had itched, sweaty in the closed tunnel, and it took all her strength not to touch it. She remembered how in the hospital they had removed all the mirrors. Six weeks later, seeing her face again for the first time, she had not been able to reconcile with this new topography. She had recurrent nightmares about it leeching off her flesh, her skin. But recently, these dreams had slunk into other shapes; they were silkier, led by a single image or feeling—a handful of moss, white roots in water, a sheet of sunlight—before vanishing.

From the bathtub she saw her phone jittering on the floor. Mother calling. She had already read the messages from that morning and ignored them. *Do you know what today is? It's one year since the attack, so you should come home. Why do you wait? What are you waiting for?*

Faint with exhaustion, Noel lay back in the bathtub. She felt a migraine coming on and closed her eyes. She wondered how it would feel to sink; to dissolve into the water, to yield.

Her skin pimpled when the bath turned cold. She stood to get out, and in the mirror she thought she saw herself fuzz, as if covered in a thin lichen. Then she was falling; the floor moved up abruptly to meet her head. A rumbling in her ears began to round out like a pebble rolling farther and farther away until she could hear nothing, her head filling with cotton.

Hours later, she woke up well rested, coiled on the towels like translucent pink fungus sprouting from the muted floors of spring.

IT HAD BEEN DAYS since the fall, and her migraines were getting worse. Noel's doctor referred her to a neurologist whose clinic was in a Chinatown building with a sticky corridor. Down the hallway were other white doors—for an acupuncturist, a Chinese herbalist, a dermatologist—around which groups of people clustered. One by one the doors opened.

Her X-ray was iron black. "Everything looks good," the neurologist said. The hairs on his head, she couldn't help noticing, resembled plump white bean sprouts—they stood from his scalp as if fat with water. His fingers too. "The only thing is that you have extra fungus in your head."

"I'm sorry?"

"Extra. Fungus." The neurologist planted the X-ray up on the light box. The sheet throbbed. "You see? Here? These very black dots? Just fungi. On average, a woman may develop two or three spores in a lifetime. You seem to have at least seven. Practically harmless. In about a decade or so, we might see some growth, which may affect the ear canal, and then we can consider surgical removal. But most choose not to go down that route. You can simply trim them with stainless steel scissors once they grow out of your ears."

Noel stared at the X-ray, the dots. She nodded mutely as the doctor wrote down a prescription for Valium, to help with the migraines.

At the front desk, she tried not to linger on the numbers on her bill. She noticed the young man taking her payment had a slip of white, like enoki, dangling from his left earlobe.

"I like your earring," she said. "Did you make that?"

"Oh—thanks." He smiled. The printer spat out her receipt, warm and dry. "No, I wish! I bought it somewhere in Europe." He looked at her, then dropped his gaze, handing her the piece of paper. Noel knew it was the scar, and she did not blame him for it. She was used to the nonstares by now.

As she was leaving the clinic, she noticed that the herbalist's office had still not opened. The men and women lined up outside were passing around a bag of pumpkin seeds. "My eczema . . . my eczema . . ." one of the women murmured.

"Neoi, if only you had listened to me the first time around," said the other woman, presumably the mother, before breaking into a stream of Cantonese.

Noel walked slower, trying to catch remnants of the language, phrases she had not heard since she was young. Her own mother had once said that she needed to teach her at least a hundred lessons a day to prepare her for life. *Neoi, don't ever go to sleep with your hair wet. Neoi Neoi, when you marry, make sure that the man loves you more; don't settle for less. Neoi, your eyes look too small when you wear eyeliner like that. Neoi, when I die, promise me you'll have a daughter so you can teach her these things. Be a good girl, now, neoi, don't disappoint me.*

WHEN SHE RETURNED HOME, Noel researched head fungus. She had heard of it before, knew that it was common in humid, hotter places like Malaysia, Singapore, Hong Kong. She vaguely remembered the fleshy growths of an older woman in her mother's apartment building at home. The woman, she was told by her mother, went mad after her philandering husband died. Day after day she sat in the lobby wearing the same lavender pajamas, using a small handheld electric fan to soothe her neck and ears. The other residents actively shunned her, and whenever they walked past, her mother would talk loudly to others as if to smother the woman with the sound of avoidance. Once though, when Noel was alone, she had looked at the woman directly. The woman stared back, curious and serene in her pastel-toned long shirt and pants, her ears steaming in the heat.

On the internet, Noel read that scientists didn't exactly know when or how brain fungi grew—its origins and causes had not yet been "concretely identified," according to Wikipedia. There were a few sentences about the lack of research and funding and multiple possible origins for the condition. A few external links took her to websites with Chinese and Japanese characters. Images multiplied on her screen: brain scans of fungal matter; women with flesh-colored fungi funneling out of their ears, woody and scalloped like lingzhi or braided with ridges like morels. There was a stock photo of a businesswoman with a bar of the straightest teeth she had seen, and in her ear—yes, there they were—lustrous caps of velvety-nude fungi, curled up on the ledge of her pinna. Another: a girl lying in a field, hair dark and parted to reveal milky gills fanning from her head. She found recipes in Thai script and hangul, which she ran through a translation system, loosely figuring that if you trimmed the shriveled edges of your fungi, you could brew the discards into a potent herbal tea with antioxidant properties. There were also murmurs of a special hallucinogenic drug with the correct extractions, professional glassware. Intrigued, she read a few long-form articles surrounding a ring of harvesters in the 1990s who plucked fungi from the ears of drugged women in Tokyo nightclubs, root and cap, and left them bleeding in bathrooms. The high, one of the convicted harvesters described later to a journalist from prison, was unlike any other. "Imagine tripping off of *someone else's brain*," they said. "We've been doing drugs wrong this whole time."

Noel looked again at her X-ray. The seven spores collected around the left side of her brain. She brushed her fingers against the area; it was still sore, tender. A soft plummy bruise was forming. She thought she felt the tissue of a growth pulsing there, close to the scars that crept over her skull.

SHE HAD NEVER NOTICED it before, but now she saw brain fungus everywhere. On the street, she found herself fixing her gaze on the ears of strangers as they passed, occasionally catching the bright shadow of an obtrusion. In Columbus Park, she wended through the elderly men and women squashed around the stone tables, red-faced and roaring at a turn of Go; the grandmas too had mushrooms in their ears, stuffed with a wispy floss of hair. It looked like the dragon's beard candy she used to have back home.

Once, on the subway, she saw a red-haired girl nonchalantly pinching and pulling at something on her skull. Occasionally, she plucked a hair out, letting it fall to the ground. After a while, she noticed Noel staring and flicked her eyes up and down quickly.

They exited the next stop together, but the redhead went first, racing up the steps. She was on her phone, whispering, but not so quietly.

"Hey, I'm coming . . . yeah. Dude, I think I saw that Asian girl that Hannah used to live with, yeah, the one who, you know, who had her face . . ."

It was bright on the streets. Light poured off the surfaces of cars like butter. She saw her face in the reflections, dozens of herself vanishing and resurfacing in the mirrored windows of the moving vehicles. She recalled wanting to die last year upon returning from the hospital after the attack.

Now, she wanted something different. *Please, please, make this easier*, she asked as her face conjured itself again and again in the reflections. *Show me how to live.*

THE ATTACK HAD HAPPENED last spring, and by the time the leaves fell to the ground her face had hardened into rivulets. That winter, she found it hard to sleep, so she would go downstairs to the dive bar on the corner to watch the late-night news and coat her stomach in thick, prickly liquor. One night there was a report on an incident down by Canal Street. A woman with meringue-whipped hair introduced the segment: "Anti-Asian hate crimes increased by nearly 150 percent in the last year . . ."

The men at the bar on their bolted-in stools had watched with slack, glazed eyes as the news footage clicked through images of streets, subway stations, the faces of those like her, composing a narrative of targeted assaults. Her scarless, smooth face was in there too, a tiny photograph like a square on a bingo card. She waited for one of the men at the bar to mutter something about how awful it all was, to shake his head, but none of the spectators moved, their eyes blinking slowly as the news changed over to sports highlights. She left soon after that.

THE FUNGI IN HER head were growing. Two weeks after she hit her head, she looked in the mirror and was shocked to see the fold of a new ear: a pale peach tip. She touched it. It felt like cloud ear fungus, rubbery, silky.

From her cabinet she removed a bamboo ear pick purchased on her last trip home. She kept it wrapped in its original padded cotton case, only sometimes opening it to admire the pristine craftmanship, buttery lines of organic wood that led to a feathery puff, like a tail. So different to the ear pick her mother had used on her: a surgical gray-and-white electronic tool with a flashlight that boiled with heat, scraping blood and crumbling wax as she screeched in pain. *Neoi ah, hold still,* her mother would snap, her fingers pulling at her ear. *You're moving too much. Stop struggling! Don't you know how difficult you're making all of this?*

She tapped the pick against the visible tip of the fungus; it did not wobble as she expected but remained firm, stubborn. Pushing the stick around the growth, she began to feel into her ear canal. When she poked the fungus, a strange disconnect occurred, similar to when she stroked an arm or foot that had gone numb. She pushed further. A loud rustling occurred. She felt something tip out.

On the floor was a small, neatly severed fungus, shaped like a small abalone. She picked it up and prodded it in the palm of her hand, admiring its color—it was lustrous and light, pink like her closed lids under the three o'clock sun.

It trembled, as if to show it had been alive, then became lifeless and still.

NOEL BEGAN TO OBSESS over these mushrooms, the mysterious neighbors in her own ear. She felt as if time was wilting, oozing. During nights when she couldn't sleep, she would turn her attention away from her bills, her work, the pain on her face, and toward the petrified mushroom that had fallen out of her ear. Using a small flashlight, she studied each crevice and cavity, the walls of the fungus magnifying and merging with the walls of her apartment. She wondered why it belonged to her, what it meant. She spent hours trawling the internet, posting questions on forums. *Are there rarer forms of fungi? Are there any connections between brain fungus and productivity? What about longevity?*

Her employer emailed, threatening that she would not be credited in his next book. She read the message twice, three times, her anxiety trying to mark a space in her body to hide and fester. But now something else was growing: something stickier and rebellious. *Fine*, she thought, *if you won't credit me, I won't do the work.*

She felt the same small resistance when her landlord sent an eviction warning. "Your tenant contract states that the landlord of this building has control over basic amenities and can turn them off at their discretion. Pay up immediately," stated the letter that was slid under her door, "or we will evict you by the end of this week."

She pushed the letter away onto her kitchen counter, the words already fading in her mind. On her phone was a Reddit thread. She had asked a question a few hours earlier, at 3 a.m.: *Does the presence of head fungus indicate long life?*

There were fourteen answers already. The first was at least four paragraphs long and primarily statistical. "It's difficult to say; the demographic most likely to develop head fungus is the Asian female, and the life expectancy of, say, a Japanese woman is already 87, compared to that of the male, which is 81 years old," it began. There were other answers that were more philosophical, ruminating on the merits of longevity. "Long life, maybe," one user stated. "But is that really what we want? Health seems more important to me."

Another: "My grandma lived till she was 101. She had the most enormous and smelly brain fungus. When she died, my dad donated them to a hospital for research, and the doctors said it was the best specimen they had ever come across."

While reading the text, she searched in her cabinet for a bag of dried shiitake she had bought on her last trip home. Each had deep white fissures across the cap. She placed ten in water, soaking them for a few hours, then ate them toaster-grilled with fat, glistening rocks of salt, scanning the internet page for clues to her own future.

THE VALIUM DEMOLISHED HER migraines but made her physically high; she felt like an oil slick. The weather had been so damp lately that she felt exhausted just from walking down the street to collect bread, some fruit. She had stopped going to the deli on the corner last year, so she had to cross two blocks to get to the Korean grocers. They were kind to her there.

The fungi grew. They drooped in translucent layers; she wore them proudly. She liked the way the growths felt on her ears, her neck, warm and familiar, eating up the sunlight and spring. She saw people staring at her. At home, she made sure to wash her ear fungi carefully in the shower. They perked up in the water.

Her mother kept calling—*come home, stop wasting your life, it's too dangerous for you there, you never pay attention, why haven't you figured anything out yet?*—but she found herself caring less and less. It felt as if her mother was describing someone who no longer existed. She noticed in herself not the familiar sensation of panicked heat, but a cool closing off, of the external world not being able to reach her.

On certain days last year she had woken up and was sure that she was already dead. That the face in the mirror was just a bleak reanimation, pale and silvery. But now she saw something else.

Look, look here.

The fungi crept around her face, breathing and breeding in her skin with a warmth she had never felt before. A skin upon her skin. Something beautiful—alive.

SHE DISCOVERED MUSHROOM SPAWN in her bathroom. They were tiny, like the holes in her skin. White slime covered the walls. She looked up how to cultivate mushrooms. Shade. Silence. Water. She made sure to always close the door, to not let any wind disturb them. And she stopped leaving her apartment.

AND AFTER ALL, WHY should she leave? After she had woken up one day last year and decided to buy some avocadoes—and then got dressed in a nice shirt just because—and then, feeling generous from the beautiful blue day, decided later she would call her mother—and then she thought of how every day in New York could feel like this, soft and glow-edged, even though there were rats glutting on trash right on the street—and then she decided to listen to a podcast as she walked, the one her boyfriend, now ex, had sent and she had been meaning to listen to all week—and then halfway down the street someone had called out to her, but she had her headphones in—and then again she heard a faint sound, and she turned—and saw a bottle, being shaken vigorously, attached to a man whose face she couldn't recall, no matter how many times the police asked, no matter how many times her mother screamed at her to remember, remember, remember—and then he had thrown a rainfall of electricity, an entire liter of acid, on her face.

Better to stay inside, with these living things that required nothing but herself, as she was. They knew about survival. She listened to them. When she drew her flesh near, she could feel them trembling, defiant, alive.

NOEL'S LANDLORD, TWO HUNDRED pounds of ham-fisted rage and hair grease, came by her apartment. He tried to push the door open when he heard her rustling around inside. But the door was seamed shut with spines of fungus, which had sprouted from the damp, split wood. She giggled. She had forgotten how good it felt to disobey.

"I'll be back," he said. "You're lucky I haven't called the police." His voice dropped as he stomped down the stairs: "Fucking Chinese. Fucking fucking chink."

She heard her neighbors come out from their apartments, including the immigrant family who lived all together, all six of them, next to her. In the middle of the night, when they flushed the toilet, she always heard the water through the walls.

Her phone was ringing but she didn't answer. When she

laughed, she felt herself vibrate. The fungus in her ears shook too.

THE MUSHROOMS WERE NOW replicating, tipping away from the walls, gilled and glass-transparent. She visited the bathroom often as it had no windows and was the best place to recover from a migraine. She liked to lie in the bathtub fully clothed, with towels lining the hard ceramic, the lights off. Often when she woke from a nap, she would sense a dampness around her, although she hadn't used any water. It felt like a mossy blanket, a protection. The mushrooms in her bathroom and in her ears liked it. They kept growing.

ANOTHER IRATE EVICTION NOTICE arrived at her door. Her mother kept calling, the voicemails piling up. An email pinged in her inbox: her employer, raging, asking her what was happening, where was all the work. The publication of his book would now be delayed, he said, and he would not transfer her payment until she explained herself.

But Noel was dreaming again. There were two closed doors, and behind one she could hear a shadow hammering, loud scratchy music, the drone of ambulances and police sirens, phone calls all hours long. The other door was quiet, still, damp.

The fungus had grown out of her ears and now enveloped her skull; crowned her scalp. Spores trailed down her neck and back. She smelled fermented, peaty, and her hands were webbed together, the tips of them growing tiny little red caps. Her eyes were moist and lined with mycelium.

She felt another migraine coming on. Two Valium down her throat. The silence coated her in relief.

In the bathroom, a colorless land waited for her. The pellucid mushrooms leaned, they curved to her flesh, the scars on her face, like a million tiny hands reaching from the rim of the bathtub. Lowering herself in, she waited for the spores to merge with every cell in her body.

Please, Get Out and Dance

Lastly, they discarded the perishables: tart green alliums; stalks of celtuce; shrimps defrosted and vein-blue; and cubed apples for Grandma, who had lost her teeth long ago. Outside, past their windows and down on the ground was a tableau vivant of foodstuff on which birds noisily descended. A family of wild boars congregated around the black-dotted bananas. From above, Frankie saw a pile of freshly shucked Spam looking like pale, dismembered tongues. She watched as people started fires in metal cans, the heat giving the air a syrupy texture, making everything resemble an oil painting, scenes already worn out.

All day long people had been holding small funerals for their books, photographs, clothing. But Frankie's family had already parsed their belongings to the bare minimum, having lived in a state of uncertainty for so long already. "Better to do it ourselves than have it all disappear one day," Grandma had said.

The volunteers said throwing the food out would help repopulate the inhospitable land with seeds and nutrients. The animals would help recreate a new biodiverse world, they explained, the wild flying ones especially, but also domesticated pets: cats, dogs, rabbits, chinchillas, hamsters, and even turtles and fish, if you could find a pond to release them into. Upon hearing this, Frankie had been grateful for once that their landlord did not accept pets and she did not, like so many of her friends, have to say yet another goodbye.

The sun was rising. A low-pitched siren began somewhere. Then each building began to emit the same noise as the clock shifted: a deep and alien wail.

Frankie had once read that music and voices with lower, deeper tones and minimal pitch variation were more comforting to the human ear. That was why lullabies played to babies and patients in palliative care were often indistinguishable, the ambient noise calling blood and flesh into deeper sleep states. A few years ago, she visited a New Age store and noticed a set of tuning forks. The sales assistant tapped the silver once on a stone and then circled it lightly around her scalp, which hummed with the same comforting frequency. "This one is 432 hertz," he said. "It's great for relaxation and peace."

Frankie thought about this as she felt these rumbling alarms, noting how her skin, her hair murmured, how her body was reacting to something she didn't know the meaning of yet. She looked at her mother, who nodded. It was time to go.

OVER THE WAIL OF the alarm, there was the resounding instruction: "Please proceed to the square and begin the day's activities. Please, get out and dance!"

Management had disabled the elevators to avoid delays, and so they walked down twenty-eight flights, hemmed in along the tight corners of the stairwell. On the fifth floor, the apartment block split into ground-level restaurants and shops. Here, a volunteer with a tiny yellow sticker on their wrist—a sign that they were to be trusted—handed slips to Frankie, her mother, and her grandmother. This indicated where they should go next: a secret destination far away from the square. The metallic clangs of industrial ventilation units covered the rattling in Frankie's chest as they left the building and slipped into an alleyway, joining cats and dogs gingerly pawing the webs of food and searching for their owners.

The alarms were louder and deeper now, seeping into their bodies like light, calling them to another place. As they left, the apartment block silvered as if veiled by a shimmering cloth. Frankie thought she saw a white dot puncturing the sky: burning, glistering. But when she looked again, it was gone.

THAT YEAR, MORE AND more buildings were disappearing, but nobody knew why or where they went. It was the beginning of the end, they suspected—soon the roads would vanish too, and the parks and ponds, and, finally, the mountains.

Several activists had warned people about this after authorities implemented a central network system that tracked and classified everything. Back then, the warning seemed no more than a hoax. But then things began to disappear. Small, unnoticeable things at first: a handlebar on the bus, a strip of yellow on the road. Glitches, just glitches, the authorities told them. But how could one explain the disappearance of a single mahjong tile from thousands of sets across the city? Or the words on one specific page of a book?

An anonymous online group found leaked data reports that taxonomized the city and began crossing out items that they could no longer find. Black ink pens. An indigenous flower species. Mailboxes. Apples. Adding them up, they concluded that the disappearances were not random. They decided that some preparation was needed.

AFTER THE VERY FIRST building disappeared, many people settled in, claiming they had nothing to hide or fear. Some migrated quietly without telling others. A third, small group—which included Frankie, her mother, and grandmother—did not want to go to America, or to England, or to any of the neighboring island-states. Nor could they stay here.

Inhabiting a small area of the deep sea had been the idea of a young urban planning student. He identified a dry pocket of air, a bump on the seafloor. He drew up where apartment blocks could be built, a little park for young children to run and play, schools for students to reinvent their futures. They would have to swim, quite far, and for a long time, but it was doable. "After all," he said, "our people came from the sea." His presentations, shown to Frankie and others in bookstores and cafés that had now all disappeared, contained slides of half-fish, half-human creatures depicted in cave drawings and ancient cloth patterns. He believed there were still fish-children living in the water, and on quiet days you could hear their voices reeding through the waves, calling to their landlocked relatives. He said, "The pearls you wear on your necks are their tears. The food you eat is their harvest. Their hair is what you boil into soups."

There was a bird's-eye rendering of the dry pocket drawn on drafting paper. Around it, the student had patched the paper with indigo squares: a constellation of water, a sky under mountain. He said, "This is where we can go."

A VOLUNTEER NETWORK OF hacktivists determined exactly when many buildings would disappear, connecting the event to the first day of the lunar new year. On this day, authorities typically organized a mass parade, and it was mandatory for everyone to appear and dance. The dancing was enforced tradition; Frankie's late father had called it "an absurdist form of soft power," one of the many ways nationalism veiled itself as culture. Before, the dancing could take any form if it was patriotic and joyful in spirit, but recently that had changed. People were beaten or arrested for dancing in ways authorities deemed seditious, and so a standardized set of steps was devised, the choreography taught to everyone in the city.

On the tenth anniversary of the implementation of the central network system, there was due to be the biggest parade ever. The date was fortuitous: In the almanac, it was considered "a good day for change."

THE SIRENS. *PLEASE PROCEED to the square and begin the day's activities of dance. Please, get out and dance!*

Frankie looked at her slip. The location of where she needed to go was somewhere up on the other side of the mountain. Better get moving.

THE JOURNEY FROM THEIR building to the departure point would take approximately five hours, and along the way they would have to hide, weaving through foliage and rock. Only a few hundred people were present, which surprised Frankie, although she couldn't tell if the others had already been caught or disappeared.

There was water everywhere from a recent rainstorm, and the peaty smell reminded Frankie of past typhoons, boarding up their windows with her father, strapping down the washing machine to the roof's railings. Living with windows was a luxury later in life. In her childhood apartment, there were none, only metal bars, and so the water seeped in constantly. In the summer months, her grandfather took her to the local public gardens, where children stuck their fingers in gushing pools fetid with half-comatose fish. The sound of that artificial waterfall, the mechanisms of a false nature, jarred in her mind as they wound through the swampy organs of the outdoors.

She listened carefully now, but she could not hear the fish-children crying. The only sound came from a barrel of macaques who were biting the legs off a picnic bench, the wood wormed to stumps.

The group reached their halfway point, a small museum in the mountain ranges x-ed for demolition, which featured a still-functional drinking fountain. They all took turns wetting their faces, water silvering on their foreheads and necks.

The museum was one of the few buildings that appeared to be exempt from disappearance and was now being reabsorbed by nature. Its exterior was clad in a thin sheet of metal that was furred with rust, and through the large atrium window Frankie saw a hanging red sculpture slowly breeding with dust and fungi. Frankie's mother and grandmother gossiped about the original owners, a wealthy collector couple who had funded the space before it was annexed by the authorities.

"I heard they moved to Belgium," said Frankie's mother, somewhat wistfully.

"比利時? What's there?"

"I don't know. Art."

"But I thought the husband is the son of some wealthy shipping guy. So, they took their money to Europe?"

"I don't know, 媽. Rich people, they move easily."

"Frankie! Don't you know someone who worked there?"

An ex. She remembered how every morning he would shave for half an hour, so careful with the blade, the cream, so that his face would be shiny and smooth. And all to sit at reception; to direct people to the bathroom; to give out thick leaflets printed on paper that cost more than his daily salary. He had been one of the first to move, settling in a small suburban town in Virginia where his aunt lived. Frankie had heard that he was no longer involved in politics or arts and he now spent his time fixing the computers and electronic devices of rich white people. She imagined him shutting down and restarting laptops, desktops, the screens blinking and blackening endlessly.

"Yes," she said, looking into the inscrutable thicket of trees ahead. "Used to."

THINGS FRANKIE HAD THROWN away a while ago: Her watch. A few pairs of shoes (inexpensive, primarily for sports). Shorts, t-shirts, a single blue dress worn at her graduation. A set of small notebooks, some cramped with looped writing, others with barely a glyph or mark in their pages. Passport photographs of her father when he was fifteen, in his early twenties, then in his fifties, just before he died. Her phone, which contained both an infinite number of memories and none at all. She had deleted everything months ago so that her screen only presented the date, time, and weather.

When she looked at her phone for the last time, she remembered distantly the memory of silly photographs of herself and her friends, screenshots of conversations, data that tracked her health and sleep patterns, and, less explicitly, where she went, how long she spent in coffee shops and public spaces, what she was buying and not buying. There had been an app that tracked her father's glucose levels, and she looked at it often, as if the last molecular remnants of him were stored in that tiny blue square. But in the end, erasing it, along with everything else, was easier than she thought. Sentimentality was a privilege when things disappeared so often.

BACK IN THE CITY, people danced colorlessly. Music streamed from every speaker. Somewhere in the crowd, a woman with a poster in her hands screamed and screamed, but nobody could hear what she was saying—the orchestra of sound was so loud—and then she was gone. How or where she went nobody knew, although the entire event was filmed live and played back to the dancing masses. Their feet flowed the same circular lines, their cheeks swollen as if bitten by mosquitoes, thousands of them stepping and hopping and arching their limbs on the enormous flat screen, where everyone looked at themselves looking at each other.

ACROSS THE OTHER SIDE of the mountain, the group reached an abandoned theme park. Dozens of kiosks were out as if on standby, some cluttered with soft toys blistering in the sun. There was trash still in the bins, flossy and gray, soft with mold. Inside, the animal enclosures—aviary cages that once held parrots and cockatoos, the faux bamboo grove that had housed two pandas—were empty, although Frankie couldn't tell how long they had been vacant.

Much earlier, when the erasures began, Frankie's grandma asked how one could tell the difference between something that had disappeared and something that had escaped. "If the escape plan was successful, hopefully you won't be able to tell," Frankie had replied.

Now, looking at the sealed cages, each one still carrying a

heavy padlock, she thought about their apartment building, the photographs and books pulverized into ash, all the obvious evidence, how humans were so attached to memory and legacy. As they walked through the zoo, she hoped to see a trace of movement, of escape. But there was nothing but empty lots, one after another.

Soon they reached a tunnel: the final passage that would lead directly to their new home. The kitschy theme park train that once ran back and forth on the tracks had vanished, and because they had been instructed to leave everything behind, there was nothing, not even a match, to guide their way in the dark. Their voices were the only way of navigation, bouncing off the algae-webbed walls, returning in a fractured singsong that told them how high and wide the space was.

Because they knew there was no one listening—no electronics to record and analyze their speech, no signals in this deep bowel of earth—the people chattered freely, speaking in and around their bodies. Frankie listened to these conversations, the rumors of old movie stars, the abruptly cancelled television shows, the songs of their youths, the days in the sun that had seemed so endless once before. She heard children asking how much longer, as if they were on a boring car trip, and couples arguing in ways that didn't sound like arguing, just words tersed out here and there. Two familiar voices wrapped around her: her mother's, velvet like the skin of a peach, and her grandmother's, sharper and edged with smoke. As she parsed through the sounds, she became aware of another voice in the tunnel, small and wet. It seemed to come from the walls, and she moved closer, the sound becoming tin-bright.

It was a song, and it was wordless, pulling into her body, filling her with a new longing. In it, she recognized sounds that had always followed her: in the water rushing into their old apartment as she played with toys of things that no longer existed; at the edges of an island she used to visit with her high school friends; in rainstorms that always came down unevenly onto the pavements, ribboned with wind; and in the water in her own body, the fluid that linked her skin to flesh, to bone. It called to her with a voice that was both her own and the history of all that had come before her. She took one step, and another, and a few more, until she could no longer feel her feet, only the gravity holding her to the earth.

THE FIRST PEOPLE OUT of the tunnel coughed, stumbled, adjusted their clothing, and then slowly unseamed their eyes to the light.

"It's here," they called back to the others. "It's really here."

As promised, there was a giant inflatable slide at least six stories tall from the mountain cliffside down to the sea. A cluster of volunteers with small radars and measuring tapes stood around testing the area. Several people laughed as they ran toward it; some were more apprehensive, approaching its edges with caution, examining the almost vertical drop-off height from a distance.

Several children had walked or carried their pets up until the last possible moment and were now refusing to let them go. A girl with her face buried in her dog's fur cried and cried, throat choked in tears. Her parents, also crying, asked her to understand that the animal would be safer on land than in the water with them. "She belongs to this world," they said. "She can't come with us. She will have so many other dogs to play with. She has all this food. She'll be okay." Frankie felt some part of her dull with pain.

"I don't want to go," Grandma said, suddenly. "No. No. I don't want to go now. Sorry. I changed my mind. It's okay. I'll just go back. I forgot . . . I left some vegetables in the back of the fridge. They'll go bad."

"Ma, we talked about this," Frankie's mother said. "We already paid for your space months ago. Remember our conversations with the students? Frankie helped organize it all. Look around you. There are other people going in too. It's okay. It's okay."

"I'll just go back! You go ahead. I can't, I can't."

"What is there to go back to? We burned everything. Everything! Do you remember? We threw out all my childhood photos. We got rid of all of Baba's things, all his clothes, his books. We had to do it. We had to do it to come here. Everything, everything is gone, it's gone." Frankie's mother had begun to cry.

"Two at a time only," the volunteer called out. "Anyone?"

WHAT IF GRANDMA stayed behind? Frankie thought. *Would she disappear too?* An old lady boiling vegetables alone in the kitchen, a crease of sunlight on her shoulder, the kettle singing, the lights all on—one day gone? Where did all these people go? And would it be worse than what they had to do now?

Relocating, moving, migrating, leaving, departing, new shores, fresh start. Frankie had heard every iteration of such goodbyes already. She thought of the people dancing in the square, how nobody had noticed yet that so many of them were absent. Bodies in the light. Bodies sweating. Innumerable bodies, replaceable bodies, drifting across land and sea.

ONE LAST MEMORY. FRANKIE tried to recall an important one, something from all the months of protest and hiding and planning, or even when she saw that corner store blink into nothing, but all she could think about was how many Sunday dinners she had missed with her family, before everything had happened, because she had decided to go to the beach or see her friends. Even after her grandfather and then her father died, she still didn't change; she would show up sometimes but rush through the food, rush through the conversation. "Ma, can you *please* hurry up?" she would say as her mother took yet another photograph of them at the table, of their plates of food, of the new serving spoon Grandma had bought that day at the market.

"One day you'll be grateful for these," her mother replied, half offended but putting her camera away.

Now, here, on the cliffside, Frankie whispered something to her grandma. A word to say she was sorry, to say that there was more to this life, to say that new photographs were being developed, that the light was blurring image into view, the shapes roping themselves into existence. To say that this all might be worth whatever came out of those pictures, even if the images were obscured, hidden from them—even if, in the end, they were barely visible.

IT WAS TIME. FRANKIE'S mother and grandmother sat on the slide holding each other. The volunteer gave them a push, and Frankie watched as the hair tie on her grandma's head flew off and her long hair unbraided into a silver carpet. The fish-children sang deep underwater as the surface of the sea met the eye of the sun.

"You're up next," said the volunteer, gesturing at Frankie.

She took off her shoes and laid them neatly on the ground next to the slide, as if to say, *I'll be back for you later.* The sky was knife-bright, the grass soft and loose, the dirt underneath still wet from rain. She dug her fingers in—it was cool, so alive—and took two fistfuls of soil and grass. She would carry this into the sea; build a new mountain there.

To My Great-Granddaughter, Who Will Find This Letter When I Am Dead

First, find uncolonized land. If that is not available, soil that is mostly left untreated—preferably even abandoned—will suffice.

When you have found this place, build a living space near it. If there is an estuary or stream nearby, make sure to fasten stilts to your home.

Once you have settled in, it is important to begin immediately preparation of the soil. With a simple tool or, even better, a bare hand, rake through the muddy earth until it is loose, tamping it down every night so that it is ready for the same process in the morning. Called repeating, this ancient practice was taught to me by my own great-grandmother when I was very small.

After several weeks of repeating, you will be ready for growth. What follows are my notes for survival. I hope you can make use of them.

THE ALCHEMY (HOW IT BEGINS)

The process of germination begins in one's head. You may start by thinking of what you want to grow. This takes some time, so be patient.

Once an idea forms in your mind, you can remove its seed. Using small, generic pharmacy tweezers and a hand mirror, pluck the fine hairs covering your ear canal. A light, gentle touch is advised. Once you have pulled several dozen hairs, you may inspect them to see if seeds have developed there. The seeds should be perfectly oval, roughly the size of a fruit fly, and glassy black in color. They should smell faintly of grass and linseed oil. If any carry fluid-filled mumpy dots, throw them away immediately—these anomalies can grow into invasive species and are harmful to the land's ecosystem as well as your psychological health.

You may bury these seeds, with your ear hairs attached, in your selected area. I recommend the patch just by the margins of your home; somewhere half shaded where the sun might slip in for a few hours a day. If you are concerned about the temperamental climate in your area, you may plant the seeds in a low, long trough and bring it inside to sleep with you at night.

After two weeks, your plant should be ready for harvesting. Extract it from the soil. When you have rinsed and cleaned out all the crevices, you may invite a few friends over and make a lavish, nourishing meal using the roots, stems, crushed leaves, and flowers, vegetables, or fruits of your labor.

Cooking with these ingredients has been a source of great joy in my life. I used to prepare extravagant feasts for acquaintances and friends, most of whom have lost loved ones, languages, lands. At the end of these meals, we would each burn an inch of our hair as a way to give something of ours back to the earth. But this was before your great-grandfather was executed, before the revolution and the persecution that followed. Before we were displaced.

One springtime before the revolution, I found lavender flowers with golf-ball stigmas growing around one of my plants. I had heard that this is a very rare occurrence, and a magical one: These flowers expand as they are cooked and can feed an entire village. It was an especially cold spring that year; I invited twenty-seven people over, and we ate those lavender flowers in aspic. Although I don't know where they all are now, I still think about our guests that day, how one woman sang for us as we cut into a mangosteen meringue pie and another showed us how to read our futures not in the stars, but by screwing a finger into the earth and seeing how the dirt clings to your flesh.

I have not been fortunate enough to find those flowers again. During the revolution, when I lived in the mountains, I made a lot of double-boiled soup from the harvests as it was the simplest way to feed and nourish a large number of guests. Many of the young people who stopped by my door at that time had no family or had been turned away by their own houses, and so oftentimes this soup would be their only source of warmth. I would set up a large cauldron on a fire outside, and while the water boiled, I would make bowls out of pulped newspaper and resin, shaped over the rocks outside my house. If more people decided to come, there would always be a bowl for them.

Double-Boiled Roots Soup with White Raix

I used to make a delicious soup with white radish, but I can no longer find that ingredient. It is much easier to source Raix, which is a canned white vegetable produced in French laboratories. It does not taste or cook the same, but it is a sufficient substitute for radish. When boiled, it turns clear and then dissolves into liquid.

Set a time for your dinner and then start preparing this dish precisely twelve hours in advance. Often, I have had to wake up in the middle of the night to start the pot, but it is worth it. At the end you will have a silky, balanced broth that stays hot even in the coldest of nights. My own grandmother taught me this double-pot method. This is also an excellent remedy for sleeping malaise, which is a condition that Western doctors now like to treat with opiates.

Recipe

Roots grown from your harvest
Radish or Raix
A slice of ginger
Dash of salt
Water
Lemon herbs (optional)

Set up a large pot or cauldron with water and place a smaller pot — empty — inside of it. The smaller pot is where the soup will be made. Start boiling the water in the large pot.

Clean the roots thoroughly but with a light touch; take care not to accidentally remove any tiny white legs. Dry on paper towels. Open a can of Raix and drain its contents into a sieve. When the water begins to boil, add the roots, Raix, a slice of ginger, and forty cups of water with a dash of salt to the smaller pot. Cover and leave for twelve hours, uninterrupted. When you next open the pot, you should have an enormously flavorful, clear broth and no remaining traces of the roots, Raix, or ginger. It is very important to not interfere with the cooking—it should be at a full boil for the entirety of the twelve hours—and it is equally important not to reduce or extend the boil time. You may serve this with hand torn lemon herbs, which imparts a sweet, morning flavor to the soup.

The people who drank this soup were younger strangers and travelers, most of whom had heard about the soup kitchen by word of mouth. Once, I fed a community choir who were crossing the mountains together; another time, a well-known political journalist found some of his former students here.

People would try to pay or give back something in exchange for the food. I have always maintained that I do not cook for money. Once, there was a man with a three-legged dog who offered me his watch, but instead I handed him a large notebook and asked him to write down a recipe for me before he left.

Later, when everyone had gone to sleep or continued their journeys through the trees, I looked at what he had written.

Thank you for the soup. I hadn't eaten anything in three days, and my dog is very ill. He is my only companion these days.

I am originally from Shuchi, so this is a dish that is popular in that region. I used to eat it all the time as a child, but I haven't had it in years. I haven't been back home in a long time. I hope you like it.

Shuchi Stem Stir-Fry

Recipe

Vegetable stems
Shuchi peppercorn
Safflower oil
Garlic
Black vinegar
Cooking wine
White sugar

Clean and rinse the stems thoroughly in spring water. Using a sharpened cleaver, finely chop the long trunks into one-inch pieces. Any browning ends should be trimmed and discarded. Keep the stems in water until you need to fry them.

Heat up a wok, without oil. While that is warming, crush five handfuls of Shuchi peppercorns in a mortar and pestle. (A note to my great-granddaughter: If you do not have these tools in the future, a laser crusher will suffice, but do not use precrushed peppercorn. It has no flavor.) When the wok is hot to touch, toss in the sediment and heat until fragrant. Remove from wok.

With a few drops of safflower oil, flash fry the stems until bright. Add slices of garlic. Add a splash of black vinegar, cooking rice wine, white sugar, and the prefried Shuchi peppercorn. You can serve this immediately or let it cool and marinate in a cold place for up to 72 hours.

I have made this many times since the man with the dog visited, especially in the summer when the heat is intolerable and very dry. The change in weather, which has only gotten worse over the years, has meant that fewer and fewer visitors came. Eventually, nobody came at all. It was me and your grandmother for a long time. I started keeping diaries.

Later, when we had to move back to the city, I would reread those diaries in our very cramped, very gray apartment and remembered how the mornings used to smell, how the birds spoke to each other. Most of the food I made came from jarred and pickled and preserved harvests from our time in the mountains.

One of your grandmother's favorite dishes when she was a child was a furu salad. Furu, if you don't know, is fermented bean curd, and the one I used was made by a woman who lived on my street when I was a young mother. Her name was Friya. She sold jars to us in exchange for translations: She wanted to write to her son but didn't know how to write in his language, and he no longer remembered hers. Friya was very skilled at many things—carpentry, painting, taming horses—but languages was not one of her skills, and for that she was mostly disregarded by the city system and couldn't find a regular office job. She sold jars of furu out of necessity; not many people remembered how to make it, and it was easy work for her. In the city, I worked part-time in an accountant's office and was a freelance translator. I paid Friya to look after your grandmother when I was away at work, and so in essence she was raised by both of us. I always considered myself to be frugal, but Friya was an artist. She had an eye for the things that were tossed away and abandoned by society. She picked up weeds nobody wanted and cleaned them lovingly, boiling the petals into fuchsia, lavender, ink-black syrups. She found ticket stubs on the street and would wet and paste them together to make new recycled papers. She liked flyers, even the government ones, because she could collect them all and with her scissors cut and stick together an entirely new journal with her own assemblages of words and images. She would make them together with your grandmother, these found poems and collages. Friya also had excellent tastebuds. She was the one who gave me this recipe.

Herbs Salad with Furu Vinaigrette

Recipe

Herbs grown from your harvest
Furu
White wine vinegar
Olive oil
Salt
Pepper

Fresh leaves are best, but if you are in a situation where that is not possible, you can use dried or preserved leaves. Rinse and rehydrate the leaves. There should be a variety of flavors and textures. Many people remove the curly tendrils that form at the base of the leaf, but I like to keep them, as they look rather pretty.

While the leaves are drying, prepare the vinaigrette by whisking a smudge of furu—not too much—with white wine vinegar, olive oil, salt, and pepper. The solution should emulsify and form a thick, fluffy dressing.

I like to serve the salad leaves undressed on a nice ceramic plate, with the furu vinaigrette in a glass saucer at the center. That way guests can dip as they please, or perhaps even eat the leaves plain, as they are wonderful and crisp on their own too.

Friya recited this recipe to me before she left. She was going to be reunited with her son. His father, she told me, had taken him across the world as a baby, and she had stayed to continue working for the revolution. Now the boy was ten years old, the revolution had failed, and Friya had been alone for a decade. She asked me if I wanted to join her. But I worried for your grandmother, who had yet to experience the constant uprooting that has come to mark my own life. I didn't want to do that to her. I know how it feels to be legless, to not have even one seed to plant something, to use the last fibers of hope you have to start anew.

The period after Friya left was very bleak. It felt as if the entire city had transformed into a giant worm, and we were eating through the endless underground, unsure of when we could resurface. Your grandmother lived her entire childhood like that, and because of that there are resentments between us. I never felt confident enough to let her out by herself.

We left the city when she was eighteen, and through an acquaintance I heard about the nomads living in the forest. A lot had changed by then; there were no more cattle, no more dairy, and most of the land's natural vegetation had been decimated by years of flash floods and fires. I taught the nomads about repeating, how to nurture the soil, how to find their own seeds, how to grow from nothing. Your grandmother and her partner adopted many of the children who needed new families. In this way, she raised a whole generation of people, who then raised another whole generation of children.

I always remember this time as the time of sweetness, of tiny shards of fading sunlight. In the summers, I would pick wild yellowberries with the youngest children, some just learning to walk, and together we would make a dessert that was very simple. We called them bedtime berries because they were always the last thing one ate in the day, so the sweet taste stayed with you all night when you were dreaming.

Bedtime Berries

Recipe

Wild berries
Rosewater
Mint
Sprinkle of sugar

Pick the berries when the sun is still warm. Clean and dry out on rocks. Place in a large bowl for sharing and pour rosewater, shredded mint, and sugar over the berries. You can eat this immediately or wait half an hour to an hour for the fruits to macerate and become even more sticky and sweet.

I must confess that I do not like desserts, but this dish is so straightforward, so direct in its innocence that I always ate it with the children, and it was almost every night that we ate this dish in the summer. In the winters, we stewed apples and made tea. We built houses. We made homes.

For twenty years we lived like that. But circumstances change quickly, and in a lifetime like mine you understand that nothing is permanent. We had seen revolutions. We saw wars. We knew of devastation.

The other day, we received news of the ceasefire being broken not far away. It was the morning of your grandmother's wedding; she was already in her long silk dress. I was meant to help her with makeup, but instead she asked me to go out and see if the harvest was ready. Already four months pregnant with your mother, she had been producing the most generous of foods: flowers and fruits and nuts and leaves the size of dinner plates, fibrous and rich. She asked me if I had experienced the same, and I told her that the day I found out I was pregnant was the day a boy soldier from my village had drowned in the lake. A suicide, they had said, and all during the pregnancy, I couldn't stop thinking about him. I wondered what world I was bringing my daughter into, how we were being so much less of ourselves—so reduced in our want for the future, the tiny holes that perforated through the dark.

Your grandmother's harvest fed us all that heavy night, and she served us in a cape I made out of fish skin. It shimmered like a pond in the moon, and I felt that it was too beautiful, too physical. Already we knew we had to move again, that there were soldiers coming our way, and I wasn't sure if I would make it this time. My dear, great-granddaughter. I imagine this letter to be like an embrace buried quick in the dirt. I am writing to you because I know how the weight feels. Sometimes it appears even the mountains possess more lightness: From where they are, they can always see both the skies and the earth.

But there are ways to regenerate. Every harvest, save a jar for when you have to move to a place with no soil, no sunlight. Be smart with where you grow, how you reinvent yourself. Carry the people you lost with you. Find new soil when you need to; build a feast when you have to leave again.

HARVEST FOR THE EVE OF A DEPARTURE

Gather all your harvest; dig up all the roots. Go to the forest. Wash the harvest in spring water. Dry leaves in the midday sun. Start a fire in a small but deep pit. Make a cover out of wood. When the fire is steady and will not fade out on you, add in the harvest, some boughs of willow, lavender, thyme, wine. Roast with the cover on for a few hours. Sit in the smoke with your loved ones. Cut an inch off your hair and give it back to the earth. Thank the ancestors for giving you this food. Begin the feast when you are ready. Eat until you are done.

The Reader

Dear reader,

If you prefer to continue this story collection in the traditional way, please feel free to turn to the next story after this one.

If you're up for a little adventure, however, please proceed to the ***next page.***

You wake up one morning and it's gone. There is a blankness inside of you: carved, scraped, dry. But you cannot name it. Everything looks the same. The unwashed cups on your bedside table, the puddle of clothes on the floor, the way the air conditioner spits a fungal mist. What is missing, you wonder? Is it your memory that has been erased? Or something else? You had heard of this happening: entire timelines wiped clean, people fading, even buildings disappearing.

You walk around your studio apartment, open some windows. It's a Sunday; outside, you hear the beginnings of brunch hour, the rush of plates, people greeting each other. All this, familiar—yet you know something is missing.

You drink some very black coffee, eat some leftover cake from a party you don't remember. The cake tastes odd; your tongue thrusts it heavily back out of your mouth. Mold. Pretty: round, stamped patterns of white. In the bathroom, you scrub your gums and the inside of your mouth until blood hits the sink enamel.

Cake from a party you don't recall, cake that is already old. How old? You check the date, but you don't feel anxious about the time. It is exactly the day you expect it to be. You go to check your journal for clues.

That's what is missing. You don't have your journal. In fact, you realize, you don't have any books at all. In your entire 150-square-foot apartment, with the foldout sofa bed, the little wobbly table, the tap that worries you at night with its dripping, not a single one. You don't even really remember what used to cram the areas above and below the television, what titles slept by your side every night. Now these shoddily constructed shelves are emptied, accented by only a few generic white candles.

No memory of books; no memory. You sit down. You don't remember having read anything at all, not in your childhood or in your adult life, which makes you so anxious you begin to pull at the skin around your thumb. You have an essay to write; you remember that.

You remember that you were supposed to write about your home. You had pitched survival and resistance through literature. The essay is for a prestigious American magazine—this you remember, because when you visualize the deadline, a spike of dread enters your gut. Then you try to think of writers who have contributed to this publication. Surely it's possible. But your mind blanks, refreshes, blanks again, in what you feel is an act of refusal or insolence. You check your phone. There are no ebooks, no saved articles, not even a single tab open. You search *book* and *reading* on all your messenger apps—nothing, not even a brief exchange with a friend. The essay is due tomorrow. You begin to breathe too quickly. How can you write, how can you even talk about survival, when you can't remember what you've read?

You try to retrace some steps to figure out what to do next. The cake is a clue of time lapsed, you know that. You probably have some form of amnesia, so the most logical thing to do is to go to the doctor's. But you are also someone who always slept with three or four books beside them in place of a warm body; every night as a child you turned pages under the covers, ruining your eyesight and your mother's patience. You stole hours at bookstores in dirty, stuffed chairs; you dedicated your life to writing, to reading, to language. The gaps in your brain are like teeth falling out, in their place giant soft holes colored in Vantablack. You falter. Perhaps you can't even function without your memory of literature.

But a small relief: So you do remember that you love to read. You can conjure scenes *of* reading; you just can't remember what was read. This gives you the strength to take the next step.

If you'd like to go straight to the doctor, please turn to ***page 62.***

If you'd like to find out where the cake came from, please turn to ***page 72.***

If you want to try and look for your lost books, please turn to the ***next page.***

The bins in the stairwell of your building are where you start, although you know you're wasting your time. If someone—or you—took the time to remove every book from your apartment, surely it would be anticlimactic to simply dump them into these grimy pits.

As expected: no books. The bins are groaning with rubbish, grease-licked plastic containers and bottles and sweat that borders on citrus-sweet. Your tongue goes cold, remembering the mold. So much trash; how can anyone remove it all? It's almost April. Soon the cockroaches will ascend from their holes and pipes, you think. You shake your head; the smell is making you dizzy.

You decide to get on some kind of public transportation, although you don't know where to go yet. The lines for the bus stop outside your apartment building are colossal, packed with hikers and families and strollers. Not the bus. At the minibus stop, you see only a few people, but when you move closer to look at the sign, a woman with long silver sleeves huffs that she's been waiting for forty minutes already. You could take the tram, your favorite mode of transportation, but you notice that the sun is already starting to melt down in the sky. And in the back of your mind, the essay, the essay.

The MTR then. Underground you go, stairs and escalators and tunnels, burrowing into the earth. Tiles and tiles and tiles. Everyone seems to be sagging, pulled down by bags and jackets and hair; no one looks you in the eye. When you sit down on the train, you notice that people are obsessively thumbing their smartphones. A man leans on the glass divider; from the other side, you see the crumpled xerox of his shoulders, his arms, the cloth bunching at his elbow. He isn't asleep, but he looks unconscious, his eyes rolling side to side. An ad plays on the tiny LED bar above everybody's heads. A slogan appears; it's one you've read many times before.

The woman next to you suddenly drops her head on your shoulder.

"Sorry, sorry," she says, horrified, waking up. Like everyone else on the train, her eyes are glazed, wet.

You wonder if you should ask if she's all right. The carriage lumbers ahead. It is so quiet that you want to speak, just to know that sound is possible.

At that moment, your phone buzzes. It's your friend L calling. L, you remember, reads as much as you do. You recall her flat full of books, spines of gold and green and red and black, just like yours.

The woman next to you readjusts her bag and looks ahead, making it clear that she will leave the train at the next stop. You feel like this is your only chance to ask her any questions you might have. Your phone continues to sing in your pocket. Above your heads, the slogan flashes again and again and again: PROTECT OUR HOME.

If you want to quickly ask the woman a question, please turn to ***page*** *77.*

If you want to answer the phone call, please turn to the ***next page.***

The voice of L has always soothed you. Perhaps it's her accent, or the way she says your name, as if she's so happy to be talking with you.

"I'm really glad you called," you say. "Something weird is happening." You turn to your right; the woman who fell asleep on your shoulder is already gone, and people are filing out of the carriage.

"Oh no, I'm so sorry to hear that. Want to talk about it?"

"It's a little difficult right now," you say. You've always hated talking on public transportation. "I'm on the MTR. Can I message you about it in a bit?"

"Yeah, sure, of course. Oh, before I forget, the reason I'm calling is I wanted to buy a copy of the book you lent me. You bought it from Pickwick Books, right? I'm having trouble finding it."

"Well," you say. "I suppose I did."

"Great, I'll go buy my own. I hope they still have it. And am I still seeing you next week?"

"I think so? I mean, yes. Where are we meeting again?"

"You're funny! I'll see you then."

You end the phone call with L. You feel strangely lonely. You wonder why. Then an urgent reminder flashes in your mind again: the essay.

You open up maps on your phone. You know where you need to go next. And you need to hurry.

*Turn to the **next page**.*

Frustratingly, your memories of specific bookstores are also erased; you can only remember one long, continuous experience of browsing, new book smells, your fingers growing damp and dusty. What was the unusual name that you just heard? You spend a few minutes scrolling online, looking up listing after listing. All of the stores are closed, permanently, except for the one that was just mentioned: Pickwick Books. It is all the way out in Kowloon.

You switch trains at the next station and continue the snaking journey across the harbor, cutting across districts you should know well, except now you have a hard time describing them. Chaotic, you think, busy. What else? Your vocabulary has been reduced to clichés.

You exit at your stop and scamper out onto the street like a mouse.

Mouse, mouse, you think—town mouse, country mouse. Where did you hear that story? *Once upon a time, there was a mouse who lived in the country. He loved eating corn and lying all day in the flowers and fields. He wore a tiny brown hat and a tiny brown waistcoat and lived in a tiny brown shed. He was very content, but still, he wanted more. He wondered what it was like in the town nearby.* Your mother must have told that story to you when you were small. There were other stories too, tales of babes in milk, of survival, of shadows between trees. *Don't be greedy, now; listen to your mother; don't bargain with the witch; two chopsticks are stronger than one; each grain of rice will be a spot on your face; don't lie, for the wolf will eat you.* You remember a red hood, a girl floating in the water, homes made of straw and sticky biscuit. Was there a story about a pig? Did she go to the market to buy garlic, or did she build a house? Or perhaps she disappeared. *I'll huff and I'll puff; I'll cry all the way home. But why have you forsaken me?* You are conflating tales with memories. You think back to the last concrete thing you saw. *Protect our home.* You hope it will not be the last thing you read.

Outside, the pavement is covered in a fine glaze; it is raining. You walk with no cover, darting around umbrella spikes and leaking awnings. You check your map every so often, watching yourself gliding erratically across the screen in a yellow dot. You're a little lost; you retrace your footsteps a few times, rerouting across grassless parks and construction sites. By the time you reach the building, the sky has blackened. Your phone glows slickly. It is 5:51. The bookstore, according to the online listing, closes at 6:00.

Not far down the road, you see a small open doorway with steps that lead down to an arcade, framed in neon. It is a familiar sight—you recall hours spent there during long, restless summers fidgety with heat, the metallic coin smell permanently smudged on your hands, reminding you constantly of this other, underground life. You already hear the *ping ping ping* of balls skittering to a beat, feet scrambling to keep time, muted, alien gunshots. You and your two cousins running around, winning all the time, the red lollipop joysticks and buttons waxy with play.

Distractions. You look back toward the direction of the

bookstore. It is now 5:55. Do you keep going forward, or do you go back to your old, underground haunt?

*If you want to visit the bookstore, and feel you have enough time, please turn to **page 58**.*

*If you would like to go to the underground arcade, please turn to the **next page**.*

*If you decide to turn back and go home, please turn to **page 76**.*

Inside, it is cold, and the stairs tunnel down into only colder worlds. The choruses—coins, winning, microwaved J-pop, hands slamming repeatedly on buttons—stream in and around you, drawing your body closer to the source of these interactions. It is disturbingly busy. Each machine is occupied by at least two people; at the popular games, four or five people, mostly male, hang off the sides, waiting with slippery, clear bags of coins or backing their bets. Simulated horses, fairies, zombies, safari lions, fish, women in military uniforms, mythological creatures, arrows and pulses, guns and batons, murderers and dancers. Bread and circuses. On the ceiling the games appear as hallucinogenic projections, blurred, crushed in a soft half-light, like the moving images by fire that cavepeople must have once seen.

There is something unsettling about the scene—how long have these people been here? Hours, days, weeks?—but the possibility of entertainment calls to you. You go through the motions and buy a bag of twenty coins from a gruff lady behind the counter, the weight in your palm tingling, and you walk the perimeter of this hazy dream space, looking for a game to play.

You see a man playing a competitive fighting game alone, the seat next to him empty. Watching, you see him win against the computer twice, three times, and the fourth time he takes a cigarette out of his pocket and lights it, his right hand never leaving the sticky console.

He turns to you and gestures impatiently to the empty seat. His expression is goading—*Well? Are you playing or not?*—and you feel both embarrassed and irritated by his invitation, as if your vulnerabilities are too obvious. You are too female, too young, too lost.

You sit, choose a character, and begin to move around on the keys, familiarizing yourself again with the game. The man's character bounces idly, waiting. When you begin to fight, you are struck back rapidly by his blows, and then you are dead. Out of the corner of your eye, you saw him perform a precise choreography on the buttons to kill you.

He gestures: *Again.* You both insert another coin. You play and die, again and again and again. You burn through your coins; you buy some more. You're not sure now if you're interested in winning anymore, but the game is safe, it feels like a comfortable palliative, and the man is a willing executor. You have a suspicion he has been there for years, waiting for moments like this. Again and again he elegantly destroys you; the ending card plays and the game restarts. You keep going. You keep dying. You can stay here, forever.

END

There is a door behind a door; and behind that second door is the bookstore. The double portal doesn't confuse you: It is how most entrances function in this city. Even in your own flat, you must open the door to leave, then a gate, then get in the lift to exit the lobby, which also has its own set of doors. *In the dark, dark woods, there was a dark, dark house. In that dark, dark house, there was a dark, dark room.*

The bookstore is empty. A woman with blue hair dressed in black is rolling down the blinds. "We're already closed," she says sternly, although you look at your phone and notice that it is still only 5:57.

"I'm so sorry; I won't be long," you say, hurrying over to the shelves. You're suddenly one of those people you swore you would never be: entitled, convinced your time is worth more than others'. But today is a personal emergency, although you don't even have the time to explain this to the woman who is now sitting behind the desk.

"Five minutes," she says, making a point to turn off the air conditioner, the music.

What are you looking for? The store is divided into sections: fiction, nonfiction, local interest, Asia, politics, economics, law, art, humor, comics. What was in the dark, dark room? A dark, dark box. You're looking for your box; you're looking for your ghosts.

You somehow manage to hyperfocus. You zero in on a shelf labeled *Fiction*. From there you can make your choice. You check your wallet—you forgot your credit card. You only have a couple hundred Hong Kong dollars, maybe not enough to buy even two books. But it's a good place to start; you need to restock your empty bookshelf. Perhaps a small jolt will recover your memory. Margaret Atwood, Han Kang, Carmen Maria Machado, Yoko Ogawa, Elena Ferrante, Mieko Kawakami. You recognize the names, but you cannot remember the contents of these books. Which will you choose?

If you would like to purchase one of these authors, please turn to ***page 70 or 81.***

If you want to keep looking, please turn to the ***next page.***

The woman behind the desk is now standing up and openly glaring at you.

"We're closed already," she says.

You feel dread begin in the shriveled, small base of your stomach. You can't leave, not yet; you haven't found a book, you don't remember anything, you can't go back home without this. You are not ready yet.

"Just one more minute," you plead. And then because you are desperate, "Is there anything you recommend?"

To your surprise, the woman seems to smile a little. Her hair glows in the dimly lit store. "Of course," she replies. She walks calmly to the back of the space and pulls out a single, thin volume in periwinkle from a shelf. "Here you go. A local author."

Somewhere in the small of your mind, you feel a memory stirring to life. Is this the book you're supposed to read?

The woman takes your money, and as you leave with the periwinkle-colored book she shuts the door behind you, so fast you feel the air push out of the store.

It is ten past six. You walk to a small local diner and order some warm food, a drink. There is no one else around yet; the waitstaff are watching the news on the flat-screen by the kitchen. Men and women in stiff, structured outfits march up and down the screen. A politician with ramen curls recites a press release. Children play with toy guns; the slogan appears again. After you have eaten and wet your lips a little, you open the book.

You are now free to peruse this collection. Of course, if you are not ready and would prefer to start over, then please turn back to ***page 45.***

Doctor Wong's office is couched within a residential building and is within walking distance, but halfway there you remember you didn't renew your health insurance policy this year.

You reach the office, unsure of whether it's wise to go in. One time, you worried about a sandy node on your breast, and the X-ray cost you a few thousand dollars; another time, you thought you were losing your leg to unbearable spasm pain, and you left with a few Xanax tablets. Doctor Wong knows you so well by now; she always asks first what is making you anxious this week. You visit her far too often, but there is something soothing in the finite clinical definitions of this small, clean space, how healing it feels even though you suspect you have an incurable sickness.

The waiting area is full of patients. A toddler plays on the old weighing scale. You give the nurse your name and take a seat. Opposite you is a poster: *We squander our health in search of wealth. We toil, we sweat, we slave; then we squander our wealth in search of health, and only find the grave.* You don't recall seeing this poster before; it seems far too ominous for a doctor's clinic, although you remember an expat once telling you how morbid it was that his neighborhood hospital faced a hillside cemetery. You felt strangely obligated to defend the city's urban planning then, but the only argument you had was for space: There simply wasn't enough. *Don't you know we live on top of ghosts?* But you knew better than to waste your breath.

The nurse calls your name, but at that moment two women enter the clinic. One is dressed in a silk shirt and shorts set, the other in a suit. They sit down across from you and look at one phone, together, their bodies pressed against each other. You can't help but notice their hair: The woman in silk is sporting a 1920s-style finger wave crop; the one in the suit has a sharply structured ponytail that reaches all the way down to her waist. They look familiar to you. The nurse calls your name, again.

If you'd like to see the doctor now, turn to ***page 68.***

If you'd like to stay and talk with the women first, turn to the ***next page.***

"I'm sorry, I feel like maybe we've met before," you say to the couple. The nurse calls you a third time, then moves on to the next patient. You can always put your name down again, later.

"Oh!" one of them says, looking at you closely, "I remember. We met at a reading last year. In that bookstore. What was the name? Pickwick Books."

"Oh yes," the suited one says. "At that local author's book launch. Terrible what happened to her. Ten years in jail."

The reading, the bookstore, the book launch. All these things that were a part of your life; their memories, vanished.

"Remind me what the title of the book was?"

"Oh, I can't remember," the woman in silk says. She turns to her partner. "Can you?"

"Ah, I can't either," the other says. "But it was an essay collection about resistance and survival through literature." Her voice drops. "I've been reading a lot of those books lately. It's the only thing we can do, you know?"

"I'm Athena, by the way." She offers her hand; you notice a constellation of thin jade and gold bands. "And this is Michelle."

You give them your name.

"What an unusual name," Michelle says.

"Yes, I haven't heard it before," Athena adds. "It's beautiful."

You tell them your mother was a poet; it's the only answer that makes sense to people who ask about your name. You do not mention your father.

"That's so interesting," Athena says. "And didn't you say you're also a writer?"

"I am. Do you write?"

"Michelle does," Athena says, pulling her ponytail toward her lap. "But not me. I'm a lawyer. She's rhyme, I'm reason."

Athena and Michelle already feel like old friends, although you wish you had thrown on something other than your threadbare t-shirt and jogging pants that morning. You are so comfortable in their presence that you feel compelled to tell them what happened. Somehow, you know it isn't just amnesia.

You tell them the story, from the beginning of what you remember: waking up, the mold, the loss.

"How strange," Athena says. "And you don't remember any books at all? Not even the ones you read as a child?"

"Nothing."

"I would try looking at a book that I might have loved before," Michelle suggests. "It could help jog your memory or something."

You're rather surprised at how nonchalantly they seem to be reacting to all of this. They're both smiling kindly, relaxed. Perhaps it's normal, you think, perhaps you're just blowing everything out of proportion. People lose specific memories all the time, right?

"Yes. Yes, I'll do that."

"Do it before all the bookstores disappear too," Athena says, still smiling.

"I'm sorry?"

"Before they close. It's almost six o'clock."

"Right." You clear your throat awkwardly. "Are you just here for a regular checkup then?"

"Oh, no, no," Athena says, laughing. "We used to live here. We're just hanging out today."

"Live . . ."

"Here." Athena says it again, but she does not elaborate, does not gesture. Here, you think, does she mean here, in the neighborhood—or in the clinic? The room compresses. Where did the nurse go?

Don't you know we live on top of ghosts?

"And you, are you pregnant? Or planning a little one?"

What?

You look around you. The child on the scales has vanished. You look for a clock, but the walls are empty except for the one poster. The desk where the nurse used to sit is vacant; on it you see a small plastic model of a uterus. Yes, of course. Doctor Wong is your gynecologist.

"Are you feeling okay?" Michelle says with concern. "You look pale all of a sudden. Perhaps you really should go in to see the doctor."

A door suddenly opens: A perfectly happy, heavily pregnant woman exits. "Thank you, doctor," she says. She waddles out of the clinic, humming, clutching her stomach.

"Now's your chance," Michelle nudges you. "Go see the doctor."

"Don't force her," Athena says. "You could also just go to the bookstore. I'm sure you'll find what you're looking for there."

You sit, your head pounding.

Do you want to listen to Athena? If so, leave the clinic now and turn to ***page 53****.*

Or perhaps you'd rather take Michelle's advice. In that case, turn to the ***next page****.*

There's also a third option: You could always just go back home. If you'd like to do that, please turn to ***page 76****.*

As you approach the doctor's office door, you hear a soft voice. "Please, wait a moment."

You wait. Turning around, you see the other patients have all disappeared.

The voice calls you in. The room is large, sumptuous, with glassy wooden shelves. The doctor sits behind a table. Her hair is so dark it almost has no definition.

"How can I help you today?"

"I'm lost," you say quietly.

"Oh, yes," the doctor replies. "I can see that. Poor thing."

"I stay up all night worrying, and then I can't do anything during the day. I can't remember anything anymore. I don't remember what year I'm in. I have migraines all the time. I feel like my head is exploding. I'm sick."

"Have you tried leaving?"

"Leaving where?"

"Leaving the city."

"I can't."

"Well, there's the door."

"I don't want to leave," you say. "I want to go home."

The doctor looks at you, her eyes flashing. She starts to write something in her small notebook, something precise and short. She sighs deeply, then brings her hand over, folding it on top of yours.

"All right," she says gently. "Here's your prescription."

You close your eyes—you are so exhausted—and when you open them, you are back in your apartment. Your books have been restored; you have all your memory back. You remember the ghosts, the heaviness of your body. You feel dead, numb.

It all comes back now.

END

In the end, you buy one book, and you return home hurriedly. You have two hours before your deadline. It's possible, you think, you can read the whole book, and then you can write the essay. You've done things like this before, surely. You have blurry memories of people emailing, messaging, asking you to file reports and essays and think pieces almost simultaneous to a political event. You don't need time to process, you convince yourself, you just have to get it done.

But you are hungry. In your kitchen, you scrounge for some leftover scraps. The vegetables look strange though, wan and ghostly. You scratch the skin of a carrot. It bleeds liquid on your chopping board. You tear open a mesh bag and find the onions have faces. A small block of tofu slides around in its carton, slippery and angry.

What happened to the women in the books of Margaret Atwood and Han Kang? you think. They became vegetables to hide from the brutality of memory, to find themselves. But then they grew only hungrier, the loneliness eating away at their flesh and bone.

In your fridge, your food whispers literature, poetry, lyric essays. *The deadline, the deadline*, they remind you.

Did you know that if you bite off your finger, it will be no more difficult than biting down on a carrot, you remember someone telling you when you were a child. *Chomp chomp. What a strange, violent thing for an adult to say*, you remember thinking. In your mind you thought not of the growth of your adolescent jaw, but of the finger itself—crunching, oozing in your mouth.

If you listen really carefully, you can hear the vegetables speaking to you.

On your countertop you peel an ear of corn reciting Theresa Hak Kyung Cha and tell it to be quiet. You shave the sugary kernels off and gnaw at the cob, unsatisfied. The fallen gold bits look like teeth; each one is singing a different ancient Chinese proverb. You find yourself licking the tips of your fingers, where the juice merges with skin. You suddenly realize what you have to do to finish your deadline.

In that first draft of blood, the iron-rich liquid streaming into your mouth, you feel moved to tears. Relief rushes into your lungs. You eat your entire pinkie, then your thumb, then all of your fingers, one by one.

END

Perhaps you made the cake. You inspect the crumbled slice: It is a citrus cake, buttery yellow and bright.

But when you look through your cupboards you see pristinely wrapped rectangles of flour, unopened tins of baking powder. Your measuring spoons are all sealed in plastic. You haven't baked in a while, not since you moved. You lived somewhere else before this. Where?

You're suddenly aware that you are in your friend's apartment. You've been here many times before. You sat on this very sofa, drinking small cans of beer. But now the flat contains all your possessions: your table, your television, your clothes. Where is your friend? Why are you here?

Your friend: She left. She planned to move to New York. Something small and quiet grieves in your body.

Now you remember.

Turn to the ***next page.***

A week ago, your friend L met you at 7-Eleven a little early, because you needed to buy some wine for a party.

"I feel like I should be buying you something a little nicer, since you're leaving," you had said, scanning the dark bottles of Australian reds.

"Don't be silly," L replied. "Any wine is good for me. I don't know what everyone else is bringing."

You wanted to tell her again how heavy you feel, but you stopped yourself. L is the fifth friend you have said goodbye to this past year. She is also your neighbor. You lived in the same building; now, you'll take over her larger apartment while she starts all over again in New York.

"Have you finished packing?"

You carry two bottles and a Pocari Sweat to the cash register.

"Almost. I sent off most of my books already. Apparently freight shipping takes up to three months."

Back at the flat, you help L prep the snacks and cups. She looks content, if not a little too relaxed for someone about to leave. "Oh, look," she says. She holds up a pamphlet for an artist's exhibition that you both visited last year. "I don't know what to do with all these leaflets." She unfolds the paper.

"Trauma fractures all timelines," she reads. "We live on top of ghosts—the ghosts of our ancestors, the ghosts of violence, the ghosts of ourselves. We exist as palimpsest. If we write, if we paint, we also erase."

"That was a depressing show."

"Yes, but I liked Sammy's new works. I wonder if they're able to come tonight."

L pours you and herself small tumblers of wine. "I'll miss you." You both drink.

The party starts when people start bursting in at the doorway. L is popular, has always been—a great friend, generous, kind, a natural organizer. You know she hasn't told many people that she is leaving, but still, so many show up: friends you know, old colleagues, complete strangers. "L," they say, "we'll miss you. We're so happy for you but we'll miss you."

The music is loud, and is turned up only louder after 10 p.m. You try to decrease the volume, afraid that the neighbors will call the police, but a woman takes your hand away from the speakers and starts dancing. She seems far too drunk to reason with. The apartment clogs up with a sweet mix of cigarette and weed smoke, and you try to find L to tell her you're going back to your apartment, you suddenly have a headache, but she keeps darting around, disappearing, her thick dark mass of hair merging with the cluster of bodies. Someone opens the windows, and short puffs of air find you, even in the center of the room. Suddenly, with more people in it, the flat seems enormous, the walls pulsing and multiplying.

You spot a mutual friend sitting on the window ledge, vaping. "Can you pass on the message to L that I'll be around in the morning? I want to see her before she leaves."

"Hmm," he says, noncommittally. He is leaning far out of the window, perhaps too far, looking down onto the street. "Maybe you should just message her. I might forget . . ."

You roll your eyes and unglue yourself from the clump of people that block the doorway. You're out, in the corridor. The lift is a relief; cold, metal, silent. When you finally get back into your own flat, ten floors down, you feel selfishly relieved you are far enough away to not hear the music at all. You've been plagued by migraines lately, especially when you read the news too much. You scrub yourself lazily in the shower, half asleep, the tiles drunkenly floating in half patterns. You knock over a stack of books as you scramble into bed, and you make sure to take some painkillers. You forget to draw the curtains, and tonight you do not put in earplugs. But still, you do not hear the sirens, or see the parade of blue, white, and red lights dancing on the surface of your ceiling. You forget to send L a text message about meeting her before she leaves. But in the end, it doesn't matter. She won't see it anyway.

This is the end of your flashback. You may go back to ***page 45****, or you may continue to read the collection, although you have been warned: Trauma fractures all timelines.*

Go home; go home; go home.

What do you mean, go home? Which home? The one you grew up in, with your family? The little apartment you now live in? Do you mean the city itself, the one that has caved in on itself? Can you really go home? Which doorway leads you there?

You must move forward. You can't go back, otherwise you'll become a ghost. Start again.

Go back to ***page 45.***

The woman is looking for something inside her bag.

"Lost something?"

She looks at you, slack-jawed. "Hah?"

"Seems like you lost something."

"Oh, no, no," she says. "Just can't find anything inside this bag." She digs a little more, the thick canvas swallowing her arm. She seems flustered now, aware of your gaze. You know you are being intrusive—it is impolite to stare at someone who is floundering, unless they ask for help.

The woman is, you feel, seconds away from tossing her bag upside down and shaking it. You've been there: rushing toward the barricades, looking for your paper-thin Octopus card, your slippery phone, your wallet. She sighs. "Can I help you?"

"Actually, I wanted to ask if you were all right," you say, trying to ignore the flatness of the woman's voice. "Everyone seems so tired today."

The train speaker chimes; you've arrived at the next stop.

"It's fine. I'm late," the woman says irritably. One last plunge: She seems to have found what she's looking for. It's a tiny electric fan, blue with translucent blades. She loops it around her neck and hurriedly pulls herself off the bench. "This is my stop, sorry."

The doors open, and immediately the two crowds converge: out and in. You see the woman squeezing herself through the portal, her bag catching on a man's arm as he tries to shoulder his way inside the carriage. Nobody is moving. The train speaker chimes frantically, and you remember how in Tokyo you watched while men in white gloves packed people into the trains, rearranging their elbows, their heads, their positions. The mass grows as more people join from the platform, pushing. The blockage starts to generate heat, and you see several figures coated in a thin gloss of sweat. You can no longer see anyone's head.

Suddenly the tide breaks and people slip like fish onto the carriage. You see the woman scrambling out onto the platform, and the broken crowd parts to reveal the station name on the walls: purple tiles, Causeway Bay.

What time is it? You check your phone. It's just past four. The train speaker beeps; you know there are precisely eighteen beeps before the carriage doors close. You know what the logical thing to do is, but it is the opposite of your instincts. You stand near the carriage doors, hearing the beeps, watching people slump on benches and press themselves against the walls. You see a man with a sun-faded tote bag; on it are the words: JE ME RÉVOLTE, DONC NOUS SOMMES. You call on your rudimentary French language skills. *I revolt, therefore we are.* But who wrote it? The bag bears a logo: Pickwick Books.

The carriage doors pull shut. You panic, you haven't made up your mind yet. But then they open again, the beeping starting over manically; someone, on another carriage, must have kept their doors open. Is it a sign for you?

Do you follow the woman? If so, please turn to the ***next page****.*

Or perhaps you'd like to continue searching for your lost books. If so, turn to ***page 53****.*

Or do you just want to go home? If that's your choice, turn to ***page 45****.*

You've already lost sight of the woman, but there is only one direction everyone is heading: up. You follow the procession, and out on the street the sun burns like your father's glare.

You don't remember it being so warm when you woke up this morning. You look at what you're wearing: all black, leggings and a t-shirt. Everyone else around you is wearing a similar uniform: dark tones, sneakers, loose athletic gear. They fill the streets. A man on a podium is speaking into a megaphone and someone passes you a strip of stickers, a poster. A crowd of people slowly march forward, all holding up one hand, five fingers outstretched. On the other side of the road, you see a group of people setting up a first aid tent, their vests bright. They're all doing something strange: One woman seems to be tipping an empty plastic bottle over, again and again. Another man is applying plasters on his arms, lining them up next to each other, one by one, although you cannot see any visible injuries. A third woman covers her face, bringing her hands over her eyes, her nose, her mouth, in a repetitive circular motion. They appear to be performing a ritual, some unspoken instruction that haunts their bodies.

You're sure this is a nightmare, but you don't know how to wake up. You want to go home. But instead you join the crowd, lift up your hand, unpeel your fingers from your fist. You look at the sky, and it is an unnatural, seamless blue. Your legs begin to move, propelling you forward. Somehow you know: This is where you live now.

END

The woman at the store seemed grateful that you bought something so quickly; she even packed it neatly in a small, yellow bag for you.

You find a small sitting-out area nearby and pick an unoccupied bench. Near you, a young couple eat their cold pastries quietly; an elderly man flings his arms up and down. There's a shih tzu, flaccid on the lap of its owner. The owner scrolls through her phone, her face blurring blue, anxious. The evening is warm like a just-boiled egg.

At the store, you had read the first paragraphs of each book before deciding your eventual purchase. Were you drawn to images of windows, of poverty, of domestic violence? Or did you wake up when you read about insidious means of state manipulation, of amnesia?

You don't have to tell us where you're at; you just have to know where you want to go.

Take your book out of the bright yellow bag, a slice of lemon in the dark scum of nonmemory. You may begin reading. Don't stop until you remember.

END

Find Your Spirit

The ghost of your dead twin sister visits you late on a Tuesday night when you're boiling ramen. In your kitchen you have three old eggs, seven packets of instant noodles, instant miso soup with crumbs of seaweed, and some softly decaying fruits that your mother gave you last month.

Just a moment ago, you had been lying in bed, the blue velvet of the hour mirroring your restlessness. You got up again. You went to the bathroom. You feel hungry, or something close to it. You haven't been sleeping well.

As the cake of noodle separates into the water, your sister's face appears.

First, she says, *you shouldn't be eating so late—it's bad for you*. Her face shimmers like a veil of milk above the starch and steam. *Second*, she continues, *download the app*.

What app?

She vanishes into the silky broth. Outside, the sun is just waking up. You wait for her to return the second night, then the next, then every day that week. But she does not appear again. You go to work as a receptionist in a dentist's office, eat the same takeaway bento boxes with squares of overcooked mackerel and rice. It rains on Friday. Soon you forget about the incident. You haven't been sleeping well.

But next Monday, precisely seven days after her visit, you receive an email with a link to a new app, free for a limited period. You read through the terms and conditions, the fine print. As you drink your coffee, bitter and hot, the app downloads on your phone. It is titled "Find Your Spirit."

YOUR SISTER IS TECHNICALLY younger than you by a few breaths, but since her death on your joint birthday last year she has remained twenty-six. At first you measured each minute and hour you were growing apart. But recently, you stopped counting. Now, you try not to fixate on the distance between you.

On social media platforms of mega-institutions and organizations, you see posts celebrating the centennial birthdays of dead authors, activists, artists, singers. It is hard to imagine one hundred. It is difficult to envision three-quarters of a century more without her, and how you must manage your own yardstick of growth, alone.

In your phone there is a tiny red dot on the date of your birthday. A standing reservation: Every year, your parents took you and your sister out for dinner at the same place. You felt it was your duty to turn up every time, but your sister was regularly late or absent altogether. Your mother did not mind. In fact, she would praise your sister's independence, her individuality, and ask you not to be upset, although you were long past that already. Still, every time you cut the cake you prepared a fourth slice, just in case.

Yesterday, your mother messaged to ask if you still wanted to celebrate your birthday. You, the eldest daughter by a few seconds, felt obligated to rally your broken family. But even thinking about that makes you feel heavy. When you do not answer, she sends another one-line text a few hours later: *Same place?*

You can't help but interpret the text as needy, even though you know your parents are struggling. Since the accident, your already-reticent father has become mute, and although your mother performs normality extremely well—she always has—you can see she is lost too.

You type and delete several sentences before sending off what you feel is a neutral response, avoiding what would have been a painful reunion. *No need for dinner this year. Thank you anyway.*

Your mother says *okay* without any punctuation, and you wonder if she is secretly relieved. You have always maintained a cool distance from your parents, although you can't quite remember who it was that initiated this.

You have always known that your parents favored your sister. They paid off her student debts early, allowed her to travel and write in America on their retirement savings. All her successes and failures defined you. Because you were the one with a middle-of-the-path degree in administration, you joined a private dental clinic and quietly sent half the paycheck to your parents every month. It all made sense in the end. Your sister died;

you are alive, and now there is money in the bank and good teeth for life. Never mind the two books of poetry you published at university, the author-professor who offered mentorship, the residency in Switzerland you had to turn down because you couldn't afford to stop working. These were all just minor things; inconsequential, really, in the world of death and spirits.

THE APP HAS ASKED for a drop of blood. The company sends you a square, thick envelope with an empty vial and a pin. This is necessary, an accompanying letter states, to accurately perform a DNA match and to prevent interdimensional connection with nonrelatives. You turn over the vial in your hand. You should have more concerns, but you don't. You prick yourself, the pin a surprising, sharp relief against your numbness.

A WEEK LATER YOU are scrolling through the options of relatives that the app offers. You see your grandparents, distant great-uncles and aunts, an estranged cousin who you didn't even know had passed away. Then you find your sister. Date of death: July 21. *Happy birthday*.

Now that you have named your target, you can track wherever your sister's spirit is, as long as she remains close to the earthly plane. Even invisible, your sister moves unpredictably, as she had always done in life. She takes her time. You note where she goes. Some days she does not appear at all, perhaps choosing instead to stay in otherworldly regions you cannot access. But over weeks you start to see a pattern. On evenings you usually find her at the pier in Sai Wan, walking between the dogs and couples and fishermen. She goes often to an old family-run restaurant in Yau Ma Tei, now managed by the young son who wears round glasses. You imagine her brushing her translucent fingers over the glassware, the greasy pots of chili oil, the industrial-sized fish tank now dry and filled with plants and vintage figurines. On several occasions you try to follow her, but by the time you arrive she is already gone—though you notice that after she visits a place, she leaves behind a puddle of water.

So you trace her on the app. To an abandoned building in Causeway Bay. An alleyway in Tai Kok Tsui. A field in Yuen Long. Occasionally, she takes the MTR back and forth between Sheung Wan and Quarry Bay, shadowing your daily commute—as a cruel joke or to punish herself, perhaps. Not once did she visit you at work when she was alive.

She regularly visits a small independent bookstore in Wan Chai. The shop is barely one hundred square feet, so you can't tell exactly what she's looking at. The location pin just shows you that she's there. One day, curious, you visit the store before work. It is quiet, and the store assistant is busy restocking titles on the shelves. There is soft, dark music playing on the speakers; posters of literary events from at least a decade ago on the walls. You recognize them from when you used to write, the names like a dream you suddenly remember.

You roam around the store, searching for signs of your sister in between browsing poetry books, zines, postcards. When you reach the local authors section, you see your poetry books and a wall of shame hits you. You try to move away quickly, but then you notice on the floor the smallest, most perfectly round puddle.

"Sorry, sorry," the shop assistant says. She toes a rag with her foot and sweeps it neatly over the pool of water.

She points upward. You squint; you haven't been sleeping well. The assistant makes an apologetic gesture.

"Our air conditioner, it drips."

THE APP'S ONE-MONTH PREMIUM service trial expires. It asks you to pay an extortionate amount of money, drawn monthly from your bank account, to continue. *If you'd like to continue using the free version*, it writes to you in faintly glistening letters, *you can do so, but this option only allows you to view your spirit within a ten-mile radius.*

Between your student debt, living expenses, and supporting your parents, you cannot afford the upgrade. You opt to continue the free trial and click on your sister's icon, a generic silhouette of a woman with flipped hair. The app tells you: *Your spirit is in Hong Kong!* You try to zoom in, but the screen sticks, breaking up into square chunks and blackness. All it can do now is tell you when your spirit is in Hong Kong and when it is not; it malfunctions every time you try anything else. The app's help chat room is useless. It is haunted by an omnipresent robot ghost who asks you what your ascendant star sign is.

A week passes, and still you check the app every day, hoping for progress. One morning the screen is a searing white blue, and you tense, nervously anticipating change. But the app is compromised. It has stifled your phone's function, and your device needs to be reset. You make an appointment on your lunch break. But just as you are turning the "out of office" sign on the door, a woman and small child appear.

"It's an emergency," the woman says, flapping at you. She has thrust her daughter to the front, and you can see in her tiny, clammy hand a bloodied tooth.

Before, you might have helped, you might have opened the doors and offered them a seat in the clinic, you might have decided to wait with them, even if it made no difference to the time the dentist actually came back. But you have grown tired of accommodating the needs of others, and this small lunch break—the only respite from a long day of phones ringing, emails to insurance companies, helping people make appointments, trying to sleep at night before the alarm goes off and it all starts all over again—is something you feel you need to protect at all costs. You can feel yourself grinding down into a heavy, blunt object, immobile, unyielding.

"You can go to the emergency room. Or come back in an hour," you say.

The woman wrings her hands, is already on the phone.

"I told you we should have gone to the other place. The receptionists here are so mean . . ."

At the Genius Bar, you are drowning in noise, blank surfaces, cords, rectangular, flat instruments with images of hummingbirds. As you wait for assistance, you recount the experience with the woman and her daughter over and over again in your mind, each time loathing yourself more.

You are shown upgrades and colors and cloud storages and payment plans, but you only crave definition, closure. The bespectacled man in a staff shirt asks if you want to delete the app. You say yes.

NOW THAT YOU CAN no longer track your sister's ghost, you have so much more time, but the days pass by harshly. The mornings are the most unbearable; you become desperate for the sun to set. Although you still can't sleep, at least it is dark and silent. You know you should take up a new activity—all the grieving manuals tell you so—but it is hard to motivate yourself, hard to enjoy even the possibility of anything you cannot share with your sister. It does not matter that in the last few years you were not as close, that her messages to you were irregular and unreliable. She is still the person who knew you the most in this world.

You go to work. You return home. You order takeout. You message your mother every three days. You lie in bed, awake. You drink some water. You sit in your shower, too tired to stand.

Then you discover that the developers behind the app have launched another version, with promises of fewer glitches and more functions. It is just as expensive, but there is another free trial for previous users. You are tempted, but this time you wait to see the reviews before you download it again. "Takes longer to load," one says, "but I like the 3D imagery."

The app has integrated Google Maps Street View into its system. You can also custom build your own avatar. You give your sister long, silky hair, which you feel she would like, as both of you have the same kinked, thick hair, cowlicks that refuse to submit. You consider blue eyes, which you know your sister desperately wanted when she was younger, but it looks too freaky. There is no shade to match your sister's actual irises. You settle on black.

You are asked to select her clothes. The last time you did this was the day before her cremation. The funeral director had casually mentioned the need for an outfit, but even that was enough to make your mother cry again. So you offered to choose. You picked a dress and a thick cable cardigan with tortoiseshell buttons, somehow worried about her feeling cold in the arctic AC of the funeral home. You felt guilty. You should have picked her favorite leather motorcycle jacket, but when you saw it hanging in the closet, you took it for yourself. It seemed a waste to burn it, even though you know this was probably what she wanted to wear to the underworld. Now it hangs in your closet, and every so often you touch it, smell it, knowing each time that you are losing a part of her, again.

You click on "Default" for the outfit. Your sister's avatar reloads on the screen dressed in athleisure.

Now you watch her on your breaks, every stolen chance you get at the office. You keep her in the drawer. You turn notifications on silent but allow the app to buzz, placing a small towel under your phone to mute the sound a little.

Your sister is touring Hong Kong. She goes to Tai O, the

small record store in Mui Wo. A beach in Sai Kung. She visits Disneyland in her yoga pants. After a while, you realize there is a logic to her itinerary: These are the special places she went to with her friends, her family, you. You think about how long it would take her to go to all the islands, every district. It makes you worry. Hong Kong is not small, but it is not endless either.

THE ROBOT SPIRIT POPS up when you click on the chat room icon. It manifests as a semitranslucent cartoon ghost, the generic sheet-with-holes kind, and spouts speech bubbles. Behind it you see the streets and road signs of Hong Kong. A red taxi cuts through its body.

How can I communicate with my spirit?

Repeatedly you write this question, almost daily, to roulette responses of vague corporate mysticism, similar to the Magic 8 Balls you and your sister played with when you were kids. "Let's ask the 8 Ball whether Alex likes you or me better," your sister would say, and you would grab at the slick black globe, muttering, "It doesn't work like that" and "I don't want to know."

Every person must charter their own path on 'Find Your Spirit', the ghost robot replies. *Can I help with anything else?*

You give up and instead just ask how to get rid of the tiny blue square that keeps appearing on the left bottom corner of the screen. The robot ghost sends you tips for troubleshooting and three pages of terms and conditions updates that you must read and sign before you can log in again.

ONE MORNING YOU WAKE up and there is an enormous pool of water in your apartment. It has crept into your bedroom, darkening the edges of your rug, shrinking yesterday's outfit into a wet heap. You check the air-conditioning units, the fridge, the bathroom, but there are no leaks from the ceiling or the walls.

You open the app, but your sister is nowhere to be found. You wait a day, two days. A week. Nothing.

You open a chat with the robot ghost, but a new ad pops up: *Changes to your Terms and Conditions: We are not held responsible for the loss or whereabouts of your subject.*

You feel a sticky rot in your chest, something hard and lumpy. You remember when you first heard the news, how your father had called and began by saying your sister was on a motorcycle, and you had laughed bitterly. You were already at the restaurant; you were wearing a new dress for your birthday, and you were annoyed that your parents and sister were late to dinner.

Then he said, "She couldn't get to the hospital in time," and somewhere in that sentence your brain split and has never quite re-formed again. After, you had this strange feeling that she was travelling, just on another working holiday in Tokyo, and she would be back in a few weeks. You had gone months without seeing each other before. That night when she appeared in the ramen, you had known she would come back again. It seemed so inevitable.

Your phone pings.

Hope you found what you're looking for! If you don't need any more help, I'm going to close this chat now.

YOU TRY NOT TO think about the app anymore. Every week or so you are compelled to check, but your sister never appears again. Your mother rings and asks if you want to have lunch, and you agree but at the last minute, cancel. You can't help her.

You are afraid of opening up your phone to news of the app being a scam, of having harvested your blood for some DNA bank that will clone you or use it for biological warfare. At work, you are blunter than usual with patients, and your colleagues start to notice. Some are sympathetic, others less so.

"She can't keep acting like this," you overhear one of them say one day in the clinic when they think you're not there.

"Leave her alone. Her sister died."

"My mother has terminal cancer, and I still try to be nice. It's just common decency."

One night, when you finally fall asleep at 4 a.m., you dream of yourself as a shadow, but not like the ones you see on television or films sliding around corners and ceilings, shape-shifting, slippery. Instead, you are so solid, so cumbersome and heavy that it feels as if you cannot move, and it takes an enormous effort to drag even one foot across the floor. You are on a quiet, light-strewn street, and you see the back of a person who looks like your sister. She moves lightly, and you know you cannot catch up. You can't even speak. The farther she walks from you, the heavier you become. You fall to your knees, and that is when you wake up, your head feeling like soaked cotton, your mouth an open O, ready to scream.

You set up the boiling pot of water again, open the same packet of ramen. When you rip open the chicken oil sachet too quickly, it slides all over your fingers, and you have to start over. You repeat the action once more, and then a third time, your anxiety spiking. You only have one more packet left.

The noodles start boiling, the scum on the surface beige and thick. Your jaw squeezes tight. The aroma of the soup summons a memory, and you try to ignore it, but it pushes its way into you anyway.

You are twelve. You and your sister sneak into the kitchen when your parents are asleep and open two cup noodles in the dark, boiling the water next to the running laundry machine so they won't hear. Your sister wants to add some long green chilis to hers, something your grandmother used to do, but she barely knows how to hold a knife.

You cut open the fridge-cold chili, taking care to pluck all its seeds out, and slice it finely for your sister. Your sister brings the two containers with boiling water to the table, but something catches on her foot—she slips—and you feel a cold-hot-sharp sensation run along the left side of your body, a shock that makes you gasp. You look down and see noodles and vegetables on your legs, your skin red and blistering.

"Oh my god, you can't do anything right," you whisper. Your sister recoils from you tearfully.

Later, when you and your sister recounted this story to your furious mother, you were pulled aside and spoken to alone.

"You know, your sister really looks up to you. I expected more."

You felt a mixture of shame and resentment. For a day or two you couldn't speak to your sister properly. But that was quickly forgotten. Back then time seemed so infinite, an accumulation of an accumulation, the days and months and years belonging to no one else but yourselves.

But not now. In the past year, you have had this meal repeatedly in the dark, alone. You scratch out the days on your calendar. You see the sun rise every morning, dragging the reluctant day up with it.

You are twenty-seven years old. Next year you will be twenty-eight. But your sister is, and will forever remain, twenty-six.

YOU GO TO DELETE the app for the second and last time but realize that you also need to erase your account. You let yourself open the charts, look at the tracked distances the dot travelled to, the avatar profile of your sister with straight hair. It's strange, but looking at this virtual person, you feel she no longer looks like your sister. She could be anyone; she could even be you. You try adjusting the hair. Straight, curly, long, short. Then the clothing. Black shirt, white shirt, dress, shorts, trousers, culottes, jumpsuit, sweater. You fix and tweak, sliding the bar to adjust your eyes, your nose, the color of your skin. The robot ghost pops up, and you swipe it away. Your mother calls, and you ignore her. You tap and press, click and slide, the hollows in your brain filling with the caulk of distraction as you try to rewrite yourself.

Patchwork Dolls

In the last few weeks with my face, I studied it closely. Every morning I ran my cold fingertips over my skin, pressing into the hollows of my skull. Closing my eyes, I tried to bind the sensation to memory. Then I performed my usual morning ablutions, washing my face, painting careful, clean decorations on my eyelids and cheeks.

The day of the surgery, Mahika came to pick me up early. In her car's cupholder was a paper bag of tiny, sugared donuts with raspberry jam and some coffee, hot and dark. "Good morning, sunshine," she said. She was smiling, and when the morning light moved through the car it slipped over the almost invisible seams on her face.

"Did you take your pills?" she asked. "They're super important. One time I forgot to take them, and I woke up too early from surgery. Had an out-of-body experience. It took me a while to recover."

"You never told me about that."

"I didn't want to scare you," Mahika said as she pulled into a narrow driveway.

There were fresh blood-red lilies at the clinic counter. We

signed in and waited on lounge chairs. Mahika picked up a few magazines.

"You're lucky," she said. "Your eyes are in season."

I looked. The last few years, everybody wanted the same eyes: domed like lemons with precise, symmetrical lashes. But now in the magazines I only saw rows of creaseless eyes flushed clean, tilted to the temples—the same eyes I had.

A nurse called the name my mother had given me and led me into a room entirely sheathed in blue PVC. There was a mirror on the ceiling, and I saw my face for the last time. The surgeon entered the room, pressed her hand on my shoulder, laid down an extra blanket on my body. I went to sleep. When I woke up, I was changed.

MAHIKA HAD SOLD HER deep-set eyes, her nose, her dimples, her lips; Jumana her sharp, symmetrical cheekbones; and Rui her high, auspicious forehead and small ears. I was swapping out my entire face. We were known as Patchwork Dolls and in our contracts—each worth thousands of dollars—we agreed to exchange our features with moneyed people seeking an upgrade to newer, trendier faces.

The name had been coined in the 1970s and referred to a method of transdermal patchworking devised by plastic surgeon Jill Anderson, which meant swapping out facial features wholesale. It was the height of second-wave feminism, and Anderson led the scientific guard, claiming that her process preserved the agency of women. She experimented and performed the surgeries on herself and others in a Spring Street loft. Her needling techniques were crude and unrefined, and she worked in thick fleshy squares, not the tissue-paper-thin, circular patterns commonly used today. You could see the delineations very clearly—visible scars around her eyes and lips like the tiny perforations on stamps—which led to her being called Doctor Patchwork in the media. The twenty-year experiment was documented in a series of photographs by her partner, the performance artist Mara Weiss. MoMA acquired them in the early 2000s.

When I looked at those photos, I noticed that Jill never changed her hair. Blond, long, straight, just past her breasts. In later images, it became clear that she started dyeing her locks to cover the gray, but otherwise, the style remained unchanged. I thought of us, the newest generation of Patchwork Dolls, the stitches glossier and finer than ever. Were there features of ourselves that we were more willing to swap out? Were there some that we would never let go?

WE MET FOR LUNCH two weeks after my surgery, Mahika, Jumana, and I. Rui was recovering from an operation the day before.

"I think she's done after this one," Jumana said.

"Like, done done?"

"Yeah. She said she's sick of the recovery periods. She has enough to start her business now anyway."

When the appetizers—rounds of heirloom tomato slathered

in olive oil and rock salt—arrived, I asked, "Do you think we only hung out together at school because the other girls hated us?"

"They didn't hate us," Jumana said. "They were scared of us. I used to hide in the music room and scratch the walls. Remember?"

"Yeah, and Miss Walker always asked me where you were," Mahika said. "Like, where's the other brown girl? Surely *you* would know."

Our lobsters, charred and dashed with lemon, were placed on the table. We had booked the restaurant two months ago, and it was a celebration of our various birthdays, which clustered around the first half of the year. Our hair was shiny, straight, Olaplexed. We began our birthday meal with a ritual of standing to measure our height against one another, something we used to do back when we all lived in Queens and dreamed of moving to Manhattan. Miraculously, we were all still around the same height. There was a wall somewhere in Jumana's family home that carried markings, like lopsided stars, of our gradient growths.

Normally, when we talked about being younger, we didn't mention how teachers always mixed me and Rui up or how one time, three girls locked me and Mahika in a cupboard and left us there during recess. Even then, I suffered from panic attacks—so extreme that my mother would pin me down with her elbows—and when the door opened again, I almost fainted with relief, light, air. Then I saw Mahika step out, and in her hand was the wire hanger for the janitor's threadbare blue jacket that had been right there all along. This was me, struggling to stay upright, and that was her: a long wire ahead, pulled straight like a tongue.

But all that was old news, and the past wasn't worth repeating. We were eating lobster; we were sitting in sunlight; we were happy, even if we no longer looked like ourselves. The money we had made was just enough to afford these meals and expensive clothes but not enough to buy houses or pay off all our student loans. The tiny yellow dancing orchids on our table made me feel rich, if only for that day.

"Oh, babe, it looks like you need to check your scar," Mahika said. "Here, let me." She took one of the restaurant's pristine white napkins and touched my face. As it came away, I saw the mucous streak. Startled, I reached up toward my ear, where a faint ache had started that morning. But Mahika pulled my hand down. "Don't touch it now. Leave it alone," she said, and like always, I listened to her.

Mahika's first operation had been years ago, although she doesn't like to be reminded of that doctor, the one in the dingy subbasement office with questionable ethics and an untraceable anesthesia process. The mattress had been covered only in a light blue sheeting, she remembered, and although she had been unconscious, she swore he had turned the television on—her dreams were full of fuzzy soap operas and daytime commercials for printer paper. After, he had proudly shown her the specimens in his fridge. There were eyes, noses, lips, a rare ear or two. Her lips were there too, a small jelly of fat and tissue resting on a sleek digital scale. Just above a pound; more than they had agreed on.

"Discrepancies occur," he had said, although he paid her the same flat rate, all in cash, no contract or papers. We all knew of many girls who had gone back to him, simply because he was fast—sometimes even operating on the same day as consultation—and paid immediately. There was a rumor, later confirmed in a cheap periodical, that his clientele was more colorful than advertised; he catered to both fetish and crime unquestionably, parcelling eyes to mafia and painted lips to men who hung them like game trophies above their bathroom mirrors.

After that ordeal, Mahika did some research and found Doctor Wong: female, younger, Ivy League schooled. Mahika's last three operations—cheeks, eyes, nose, in that order—had taken place in Doctor Wong's Upper East Side clinic, a noticeably fridgeless place. Doctor Wong took a 30 percent cut, but that was totally reasonable, Mahika said, considering the health risks involved and the clinic's notoriety for discretion. The purchasing clients could select their desired features from categorized databases, but the seller would not be privy to any of this information. Transactions were, to an outside view, clean and closed. But there was one telltale clue. Because Doctor Wong had trained under a doctor who followed in the school of Jill Anderson, her contracts included a legal name change to indicate our status as "plastic donors"—although, of course, the media and everyone else always called us Patchwork Dolls, or PDs. This was how Mahika Nair became Mahika PD Nair, and how

I, a few months before my twenty-eighth birthday, became Sophia PD Leung.

In that first week after my surgery, Mahika took me to Chelsea Market to pick out some salmon fillets, something we had never previously allowed ourselves to buy. In the aisles we imagined the feasts and banquets we would make for our friends, how we would load platters of shaved truffle and garlic-fried ramps and whole cumin-roasted lamb onto the tables of our duplexes and mansions. With our new faces—mine still bandaged—we tasted squares of peach, kettle chips infused with rosemary and jalapeño. Then, as we neared the cold counters, she pulled me aside, whispering. Her eyes were on a brunette woman in leggings and a jogging bra by the salad bar, picking out kale leaves into a tub. It seemed as if she were using the tongs as tweezers, and she inspected each leaf for a few seconds before dropping it slowly into the container. We watched for a while, and I commented amusedly that the woman seemed very fastidious in her selections.

"No," Mahika said, "she's had the surgery. I think she's lost her depth perception."

I looked again. I couldn't see any visible scars on the woman's face, but the areas around her eyes seemed vaguely mismatched in tone, as if bleached by the sun. "How do you know?"

Mahika laughed, but it sounded like the laugh my mother used to make when she heard news about her hometown in China on the radio. We continued quietly through to the beds of ice, the limp, shiny fish, and molluscs with shells, stinking high of another kingdom. Everything shone as if coated in an inky glaze. After we left the market and got back into Mahika's car, she finally turned to me and said, "I'm pretty certain, Sophia."

"Certain of what?"

"You can't tell? After all these years?"

"Certain of what?" I grew impatient. She fumbled in her bag, and I thought she was looking for her keys, but instead she took out a pair of sunglasses she had bought recently in Seoul. They were oval, sleek, but the way she put them on shakily made her look comical, like a pop star caught in the crosshairs of camera flashes.

"That woman," she said finally. "She has my old eyes."

SOMEWHERE BETWEEN JILL ANDERSON and Doctor Wong, transdermal patchworking had become taboo, then radical, then taboo again, and now it was a nationwide, money-making industry that entangled dozens of doctors and hundreds of women. There were investigative essays. There were opinion pieces written by women—on both ends of the transaction—who were grateful for the legality of the procedure, others who regretted their surgeries. *Slate* published an anonymous tell-all by someone who worked at a pharmaceutical conglomerate, claiming that big pharma industries were making billions off of these surgeries and their collateral medications, foundations, toners, and diamond sandpaper smoothers. The past few years had seen heightened discourse around the murky racial inequities embedded in current practices, with people pointing out that the majority of buyers were affluent white women dabbling in ethnically ambiguous faces, and the sellers were primarily disadvantaged women of color. Academic papers on the topic surfaced on JSTOR, dissecting hauntological theories around why we, as children of immigrants, were doomed to sell ourselves, and how colonialism presented itself in the purchasing of such flesh. Social media couldn't decide where the fault lines lay. Some strangers weighed in sympathetically, noting that while the buyer could flaunt their upgraded features, the seller could only hope to assimilate to their haphazardly cut-and-paste bodies, made up of buyers' discards. At best, we were just victims. At worst, they accused us of complicity in modern slavery, profiting off oppression and undoing years of intersectional feminism.

These accusations were hard for me, because the truth was none of us had heard about Patchwork Dolls until Mahika met Hattie. Hattie was deer-limbed, red-haired, and operated like all great orators did, with equal measures charm and tyranny. She was in Mahika's gender studies class at college, and within days of their meeting they became a couple and moved in together. Three months in, Mahika found the documents and papers on Hattie's desk.

"What's this?"

"Mm? Oh, nothing, just some research. Have you ever heard of Jill Anderson?"

It was eight years ago. A revival of PD practices was in motion after a long drought—in the 1990s, Anderson had been found guilty of malpractice by a board of male doctors, and she had her medical license revoked. The thing they stuck her with, Hattie explained to all of us, was her lax approach to patient-doctor confidentiality. She pushed forward Anderson's memoir, which contained dozens of case studies. But it was unjust, she told us. She was a pioneering queer feminist. She helped hundreds of women. And those men? They targeted her because they didn't like that. As women, we have to highlight the injustice of this treatment.

In between classes and lecture halls, I would join the occasional march. I had never seen Mahika look so happy. I'll always remember her old face in those days, sweaty, shouting, a sun all in itself.

As for myself, I thought I was being a good friend, holding a picket sign every once in a while, talking to Mahika while she printed flyers in the library. Generally, though, I really tried to stay out of it—I also hadn't joined the college debate team, or the nascent, small activist groups on campus. It was something my mother had taught me: Don't make waves, but ride them if you need to.

Everything became complicated. Hattie would tell us that in order to radicalize our political selves, we had to give in to the system and then subvert it; then she would tell us that by being complicit in a system, we were denying others the rights to choose. I would see others slide close to her, then fall away, like a circle waxing and waning, her at the boiling center. I don't think we ever stopped to think why we were following orders given by someone who looked nothing like us: someone who had spent her summers in a five-bedroom lake house upstate and whose parents were on museum boards; who protested injustice with obscure theoretical Instagram posts written while she listened to experimental ska on her vintage speakers; who never asked who we were before we met her; who never was able to unpeel our identity from how we looked. It all felt twisted, but it was thrilling too, a drama that we could, on good days, distance ourselves from, and on bad days shroud ourselves in. So we followed her nonetheless, my old, dear childhood friend Mahika now the meekest, tamest of us all.

When Hattie suggested that they swap their lips, Mahika called me.

"I'm so excited," she said. "I've always hated my big lips. Hattie already found someone. He said he can do it soon, like tomorrow."

"No," I said, "don't do it." And I would still say the same thing today.

Mahika hung up. Later I wondered how Hattie had proposed this to her. Had there been something romantic, electric, to the suggestion? Had it been brought up over dinner, over wine, while they had been kissing, sucking each other's lips, wondering what it would be like to kiss yourself, to love yourself? Was it a pity transaction—Mahika embodying charity—an act of mutual witness or self-loathing? Lust or envy?

Even Mahika seemed to know that after the surgery Hattie would disappear. "Her life is about controlling people like us," she said bitterly to me, "since she can't accept the fact that she was born so rich, so white, and so ordinary." Later, I discovered

Hattie had been romantically involved with multiple people, and she orchestrated the same dance, holding power over several small groups of friends at the same time, knowing that we were loyal to one another, even when those friendships became toxic. Her vanishing was a relief. It seemed like a hat trick, a Gordian knot that wrestled loose at the magician's touch.

The week after we were free of Hattie's influence, Mahika seemed to revert instantly back to her old self and furiously researched a new doctor who could fix her botched lips. A few months later, Jumana and Rui signed up. I was the last one, not because I was apprehensive of the surgery, but because I still wasn't sure how to trust my own morals, my own instincts. Following Hattie had been easier. The discomfort had only briefly clashed with the addiction of belonging to something larger than ourselves. Maybe that's why I eventually signed up for the program; not because I had figured everything out, but because even then I was still in that cupboard, waiting for Mahika to open the door. And I saw how my friends changed with the money, how much more they could breathe after paying off huge chunks of student loans. How easy it was to walk past a boutique and buy something, to regulate routines of self-care, to settle rent and plan a holiday on the same day, to be able to pay for others to cook for me and wash my hair and fix my teeth. As I prepared for my surgery, I privately said goodbye to the parts of myself that had once seemed so special, so unique, and then compartmentalized them down to icons on a screen, something with a tiny little price tag that a buyer could click on.

When I received my first check, I took a photograph and sent it to our group chat. *Drinks on me tonight*, I wrote. *Also, I really want to check out that new Korean fine-dining restaurant that just opened!*

My face hurt, everything hurt, but I could drink through a paper straw and eat soft foods if I parted my lips very slowly and dribbled something inside with a spoon. My friends, with their salon-fresh hair and new lips, eyes, foreheads, cheeks, noses, and chins, congratulated me and drank and ate more on my behalf. I kept expecting Hattie to suddenly show up, and once I even lifted my head after hearing a voice that sounded like hers. But there was nothing in front of me except the thronging crowd of a packed bar, and a wide, oily mirror that reflected back my bandaged face, blurred and bright in the velvet shadows.

MY BODY WAS REJECTING my new face. There was a 0.005 percent chance of it happening, but it was undeniable: My new skin was clamoring to get out. In the mornings I felt my flesh melting off of my skull; I had to use my palms to push it back in, and when my fingers came away they were coated in a rusty discharge. My eyesight deteriorated, but most of all it was difficult to breathe. I found it hard to move my new lips, not knowing which muscles to use, and everything kept sliding around. Sounds felt like hollow thuds in my ears. Every day I went through multiple rolls of bandages. I wondered if the woman who had my face was reacting the same way, if she was suffering as I was.

I called the clinic, and they asked me to come by immediately. Doctor Wong was waiting for me in a room I hadn't been in before, along with a nurse, a lawyer, and a woman pouring out increasingly burnt coffee. It smelled like motor oil and hand soap.

"I can assure you this has never happened before in my clinic," Doctor Wong said.

The lawyer in the room chirped, "And you agreed to the risks when you signed your contract."

I didn't understand what they meant at first, but then I looked at their faces and realized they were telling me I couldn't sue.

"I just want to know how to fix this."

"There's some medication we can prescribe," the nurse said. "Also, you may need to come in for some tests."

Doctor Wong walked over to my side of the table and sat down next to me. "May I?" She gestured to my face, which I had bandaged that morning in a fine wheat-colored gauze, clear enough so that I could see, but layered in ways that abstracted what was beneath it. Sometimes I saw girls shopping together at Sephora or Brandy Melville with these coverings. So young. I wondered how long their friendships would last.

I nodded to Doctor Wong, and she began peeling at the small, knotted nub at my chin. At the fresh contact with air, my new skin began to burn, tiny blistering pulses that itched at the seams. She frowned.

"How long?"

"It's been this way since the surgery, so about a month. I just thought it was part of the recovery."

"You should have called us right away. Didn't you read the instructions in your booklet?"

I recalled Mahika telling me that I didn't need to read that stuff, that she would tell me everything. For the past week, I hadn't been able to reach her though, but that was normal—sometimes she would turn off her phone for a while without telling us, and when she came back online, she would say it was a necessary break from us, from everything. My mother had died during one of these disappearances. I had learned to stop being angry at her, to stop depending on my friends so much. "We have each other, right?" Mahika would say to me, and I always knew she meant only on her terms.

Doctor Wong made me sign more papers. I looked over them all carefully, but it wasn't as if I had much of a choice. She would have to perform more surgeries, she said. It was worse than she thought.

"You might notice that your face will be slightly larger. That's because I need to graft another layer, which will help you develop thicker skin. This extra surgery can be subsidized by the clinic and the fees paid by the client, but I'm afraid you will need to pay for your medication, which we cannot provide. I will warn you now that it is expensive. You can give the prescriptions to a pharmacy."

I had already spent half the money on paying off a lump of my student loans and frivolous things like clothes, jewelry, expensive meals. I knew I looked terrible whenever I left the house, but as long as I kept eating good food and drinking good wine, I could convince myself I was living, that I was making a good life. I was considering a trip to Spain the second my face cleared up. But when I realized nothing was clearing up, I called the clinic. In my head I calculated the costs of it all. If I sold something else, like my breasts or my feet, I could get back on track. Doctor Wong did not offer those services—she only did faces—but I knew there were a dozen or so unlicensed clinics, just like the one Mahika first went to, around the city.

"Isn't there anything else I can do?"

Doctor Wong leaned forward in her chair. "I've only seen one case of this before, when I was an intern. Want to know what happened to the girl?"

I nodded.

"You know how if you scrape yourself, your body grows new skin in that area? The girl started growing another face underneath her new one. So, we had two choices: Either we removed the new face, or we had to stop the secondary one from growing. But by the time we realized this, it was already too late. The girl died. She was trapped in her own face."

Doctor Wong put her hand over mine. "Sophia. You don't want to be like that girl."

WHEN I WAS TWELVE, a boy broke my nose in the school courtyard by pushing me off the steps. His hand had appeared not on my bag or my hair, but on the thin bone of my shoulder, his fingers pressing dangerously into my clavicle. Seven pounds of pressure and it breaks, that bone, I found out later. If the boy had been bigger, older, fleshier, the weight of his arm alone could have shattered me. But instead he used gravity, and I fell down the steps onto my nose, twelve years old, the gravel salting my skin.

Later, Rui suggested he had a crush on me; that to touch me, however violently, was a gesture of the shame that had developed from his desire. I asked her how she knew, and she said she overheard the boys ranking the girls in the class, and the one who said Sophia was laughed at. The other boys said, "Who, that Chinese monkey?"

The woman who now has my old face does not know this story. She does not know, either, of how when I was twenty-one, a man followed me home and tried to rush me at my building door, and I, screaming, threw a fistful of coins to escape; later, I saw his face on the news along with tiny postcard stamp photos of other Asian women. She does not remember how it felt to have my mother poke my head with a pencil during study sessions, or the way my grandma would inspect the proportions of my face by measuring it with a ruler, muttering about bad superstitions. With money earned from my first part-time job I drew exaggerated inked arrows on the outer corners of my eyes to make them appear larger; around that time, an older, male colleague told me I had perfect hentai face potential. For my twentieth birthday, just before she died, my mother gifted me a costly snail mucin cream from Korea that turned out to contain flesh-festering levels of bleach. Padded bras, leg shiners, thigh binders, blepharoplasty, chin firmers, fillers, perms and straighteners.

Movies and pornographies about women that looked like me, sex dolls, doxxing, feminism. On a white woman, my face was desired, ambiguous, a symbol of power and wealth. But for me, it had been a curse, something I desperately tried to scrub out. I had been forcing my body to adapt for so many years—to witness the wretched ornamentation of my being—that this new suffering seemed an appropriate response. Finally, it was trying to wriggle free: enough, enough, enough.

But still, I wanted more. I wanted Spain. I wanted sunlight. I wanted to eat at good restaurants. I wanted to feel less alone. I just wanted simple things, not to change the world, I told myself as I took the pills, prepared for the extra surgeries, texted people I had always avoided, who knew where these darker, damper rooms of frozen body parts were. If this was the cost of living well, if this was the currency the world accepted, I could learn to accept it too. My body would forgive me. It always has.

THE NEXT TIME I saw Mahika, I was four weeks into my medication, two weeks from the last facial reconstruction Doctor Wong performed, and five days out from the other surgeries. My body was refusing to settle, but my attempts to placate it with a grotesque amount of drugs seemed to be working. Occasionally something in my veins bleated, my flesh curled, but then I took another pill and it went dead, silent. We met up at a small Egyptian café in the West Village and had pastries. I didn't bring up my ordeal, and she didn't ask. When she saw the medication in my bag, I just told her they were all necessary for recovery.

"I went out for lunch with her," Mahika said.

"Who?"

"The woman who has my old eyes. The one we saw in Chelsea Market."

I was quiet.

"I went back there a week later at the same time, around lunchtime. She was there again. She works in the area as a gallery assistant."

"Is that allowed?"

"I don't see why not," Mahika said. "There's nothing in our contracts that says we can't interact with them if we happen to run into one of them in public."

"Did she confirm she's a PD?"

Mahika paused. "No," she said.

"Did she recognize you?"

She sighed. "No. I just sat there like an idiot, hoping she would bring it up or notice that I had her old eyes, but she just kept talking about work and her boyfriend. I tried to look at her name when she handed over her credit card, but then I remembered that clients aren't obligated to include PD in their names. Only donors."

My mouth was moving faster than my brain. "There's something weird about you meeting up with her," I said. "It doesn't feel right."

"You're really questioning the ethics of this?"

"I don't know. It just feels wrong." I felt the wind on my skin, turning cold.

"I mean, what would you do? If you saw someone with your old face?"

The truth was that I did not like thinking about the woman on the other end of the transaction. I did not want to confront why she had chosen to appropriate my face, out of all the others in the dozens of binders at Doctor Wong's clinic. The image haunted me, and I pushed it away every time.

But Mahika didn't push anything away. I had seen her get into fights at school with girls who cut her hair and stuck used sanitary towels onto her backpack. I liked when she stood up for us, admired her directness, but not when her accusations were pointed at me. I knew she was calling me weak, that I was a hypocrite, I could hear it in her voice. This was our friendship: a tug here, a tug there, trying not to unravel what was in the weave.

"Why did you get the surgery?" she asked.

"The money." I answered this so immediately I surprised myself.

"That's it? So practical."

"What do you want me to say? I'm fighting the system?"

"I think we owe it to ourselves to figure out how we play a role in all of this."

"I'm not sure if that's our responsibility," I countered. "I'm just someone who made a choice, and maybe it was a bad one, but I can live with that." I knew I sounded defensive, that Mahika didn't even know about all the other surgeries, but I needed to protect myself, to tell my body that this was the path I had taken.

"I hope you don't really think that," Mahika said. "I hope

you're thinking about your purpose more seriously. You know there's more we can do."

"More?"

"We're icons, Sophia."

She plucked a yellow poster out of her bag. It contained instructions to bring comfortable shoes, bottles of water, and picket signs. The destination was Doctor Wong's clinic.

"One of the girls at the nail salon gave it to me. It's a rally for women of color to fight for the rights of Patchwork Dolls. They're targeting all the PD clinics, including ours, and they're going to demand client transparency. Why shouldn't we know the white women who have our faces, the people benefiting from what we had to grow up with, what we endured to get here? Don't you sometimes feel like we're just being used in this giant, abstract plan? Don't you want to at least try and fight against all that?"

"Mahika," I said. "I'm really tired. The medication? It's expensive. And it makes me sleep fourteen, fifteen hours. Then I have to work. I don't think I have time for this."

"Rui and Jumana are coming," she said. "I already told them about it."

I repeated myself, although I knew we had eased back into a familiar, uncomfortable dynamic: "I don't think I can make time for this."

"It's on a Saturday—surely you don't have to work then? And maybe we can come over to make some posters the night before. You have a giant apartment. You should use it for something."

Mahika had always been very good at this: making you feel bad about certain privileges you earned, the money you made, the things you tried to protect for yourself. I knew it had something to do with Hattie and all the therapy she had been to as a consequence—all the squares on social media telling her to demand more, to practice wellness for oneself, to be selfish. I understood all this. It was one of the only reasons I had any sympathy for her still.

"My apartment is big because my mother died and it was passed down to me, her only child," I said. "I don't know what you want to me say."

"That you'll come."

"I can't. No."

I saw Mahika working something out in her mind.

"All right. You can come to the next one then."

Our tiny espressos arrived, with cookies wedged in the cup handles. We swirled them around in the dark liquid, the crumbs sugary and gold. Mahika paid the bill, then gave me a look that I still can't figure out, no matter how many times I've gone over that interaction in my mind. I thought of the wire hanger she so meticulously untangled, how she knew exactly how to angle it in the keyhole of the cupboard. Mahika and I measuring ourselves on the wall of Jumana's old house, our heights never too far from each other, a comfort and a threat. It scared me, her precision, how she knew exactly what to do, what our paths should be. She would often remind us of how she saved me, and how we were all, now, connected through these surgeries. But I could no longer follow her; I had already come apart and needed to find my own way out. She got up to leave.

"Get some rest, Sophia. You look awful."

IN THE YEAR AFTER they vanished from my life, I would see them on the television, my old friends with their new faces. Over time, the small rallies became a larger movement, and violent factions formed. They smashed and robbed clinics, some even selling body parts to the black market so that they could raise more funds for their cause. I knew this was a toxic cycle. I wanted no part of it.

My body, as I had hoped, learned to assimilate and live with the trauma. Once or twice a week I woke at night and felt myself separating, as if my flesh was radiating a homing signal to the other parts of me that were gone, but the phantom loss was easily squashed with a few more pills. When I showered, my newer parts felt chunkier, heavier, although overall I had lost a few pounds. At first, I panicked that somewhere there was a stitch undone, a patch loose, and moisture was getting in. But after I dried off, I would usually forget those anxieties when I looked at myself in the mirror, the boiling temperature of the water temporarily revealing the hairline fissures on my body, the swath of skin that was pinker and puckered with white, the two new, pale moons on my chest.

When I was outside, there was little pain. Acquaintances remarked on my appearance with a slightly strained, yet encouraging tone one might use to register an unsettling change: *Wow, is your—did you—change your hair?*

I went to Barcelona and ate octopus every day, a dozen different ways: fried, stuffed, in olive oil, smothered in paprika, inky and dark. I drank wine alone in bars; I wrote postcards to myself. I bought fruit from the market, pretending I was a local, although the men looked at me strangely—as if they couldn't decide what kind of thing I was: a person, or an approximation of a person. I visited Gaudí's Casa Batlló, the house of bones. Wherever I turned, there were curvilinear walls, windows like translucent cells, uneven floors that made you seasick. I read that Gaudí had designed the house to be devoid of any straight lines. It felt like the lining of a soft organ—not like bones at all, the only things, perhaps, in my body that I couldn't ever change.

When I returned to New York, I tried to be kinder to myself. I painted the walls of my apartment seafoam green in the spring. I put up photographs of my dead mother. I took calcium pills.

The movement was still going strong. The last I heard, Mahika, Rui, and Jumana were moving around the country but mainly stayed close to Seattle, where every year there was a giant global medical conference. I followed the news, and sometimes when I saw one of my friends, I would gaze at them passively, like how I used to read all those articles that were about me but also not about me. I saw that Mahika had changed her name; people were calling her a doctor of some sort, and she dropped the PD.

I kept my name because it cost money to change it, and because I wanted a concrete reminder of that time. I needed a marker to move on from. Whenever I was at the post office or the hospital and someone called out Sophia PD Leung, people would turn to look at me, but then their attention drifted away, as if disappointed by how ordinary I seemed. I wasn't an activist or a feminist or an icon—I was just myself, with slightly more money than before and a history of bad choices.

Without my friends, I went to brunch. I went to happy hour. I booked trips to Kyoto, to Niagara Falls, to Paris, to my mother's home city in China, and then back again. I listened to new music; I watched new films; I found ways to keep refreshing, like a browser window, in a world that was always changing.

Galatea

At the apartment, the man points to the sofa and you obey, taking off your shoes. In front of you is a knockoff Noguchi table and two identical candles. He asks what you think of his place, and you say, "It's nice," although you aren't sure yet. You have been on four or five mediocre dates with him, but this is your first time at his apartment.

The man sits on the other end of the sofa, and you wonder when he will attempt to undress you, how the awkward lurch or fumble will begin, but he shows no movement at all, sitting as far away as possible. He pours you some wine and his hand hovers, for too long, over a candle flame. You realize it is artificial: a smokeless pillar with a wriggling tab.

"You have fake candles," you say neutrally.

"Yes," he replies. "Actually, I prefer them. Sometimes fake things are better than real, right? The light lasts forever and there's no risk."

As he says this, you notice there are two pianos in the room: a silent baby grand and a self-playing one, the keys moving on their own as if by the pressure of invisible fingertips. He pours more wine, the sound cantering with the music.

Before meeting this man, you had all but given up on dating.

Now, he suggests rote companionship; you could spend dozens of evenings watching tastefully pornographic art house films, ordering omakase menus at tiny restaurants, booking the occasional long weekend in Tokyo or London. You are thirty-two years old, after all. Your colleagues remind you often of your limited options.

You excuse yourself to the bathroom and find more fake candles and an M. C. Escher print, a box of USB sticks by the sink. You pee sluggishly, exhausted already.

You return to the living room.

"Smoke?"

The man has opened the balcony doors, and a new smell enters the room, damp and fragrant and salt. You suck it into your lungs.

There is an artificial waterway near the man's apartment. In the summer, people like to pull on their long-sleeved bathing suits and sit on beds of sand drinking cantaloupe juice. Sometimes, when it is very hot, blankets of sulphur float in from the plastic molding factory situated further upstream.

Early spring is when you like to visit the river. It is usually very cold, but with your body wrapped in wool you can walk for hours. When you return home, your toes, your eyes, your ears are singed with cold. And for a short while, as you warm up, your cheeks bloodred, it feels as if you are changing. But the next day arrives, and then the next, your walks by the water grow warmer, and soon it is sweltering again. You join a dating app, message a few people, have a few lackluster dinners, delete the app. You buy a new summer dress and hang it up alongside all of your other thin, long dresses. Time passes, but nobody seems to notice except you. You aren't even sure you're processing anything; you're just observing. When you look back at photographs of yourself by the river, you even notice the same vendors in the background, the same dogs wearing glow rings on their necks. Everything you do feels copied and pasted, templated from another life.

OUTSIDE ON THE BALCONY at the man's apartment, the air is colder than you expect. It is only then you realize that you're drunk—how many glasses of wine have you had since you arrived? Three? Four?—and your face flushes against the bracing wind.

The man's balcony is wide and new, just like everything inside the apartment. There are two deck chairs, a rattan sofa set with blankets and pillows, a small, circular table, a half-yellowed monstera plant. The man fumbles with some cords, switches on a heater and two garden lamps. Outside, he seems rougher, sharpened by the temperature drop. He lights a cigarette, puffs on it a little, asks if you're cold. Without waiting for an answer, he pulls a blanket off the sofa, handing it to you. You take it and then notice that where the blanket was there is a large shape, hands, a face. You feel the blood leave your body.

"Don't be alarmed," he says quickly. "She's not real."

You let out two, four, six gasps, clutching the blanket to your chest. A metal-bitter taste in your throat. Immediately you can see that the woman isn't real—she's just a wax figure—but still there are spots behind your eyes, a clamoring in your belly. You laugh a little to relieve the tension. The man is watching you carefully.

To calm yourself, you begin to study the figure, just like when you were a child and you saw something in the dark. To see the shape of something, you realized, was to understand it better—a lamp bent strange in the shadows, a piece of paper wilted on the floor.

The figure before you has poreless, lucid skin and dark, very shiny hair that comes together in a low bun at the nape of her neck. Her eyes are soft and wet.

"A friend manufactures these dolls in Zhongshan," the man explains, then hastily adds: "She's not a sex toy, if that's what you're thinking. More for companionship."

A CompanionDoll. The company that makes them is emerging but powerful in financial and public backing. They claim that their dolls not only appear lifelike, but are also capable of emotional maturity. You read recently in a newspaper that the CEO has plans to collaborate with the government. He mentions that his vision for restructuring labor forces would eliminate the need for migrant workers and caretakers, reducing costs and prioritizing efficiency. But for now, the CompanionDolls are still in test mode—a public beta. You see them milling around in pairs or threes at giant chain restaurants, hospitals, care facilities for the elderly, wearing blue uniforms and dead-eyed, glassy stares.

But the one in front of you is different. She is alone. She wears a standard charcoal gray sleeveless dress, a white gauze scarf at her throat. You catch pearls on her ears, slingbacks with inch-and-a-half heels. She does not look like the others. She looks, you realize, like a generic female office worker. She looks like you.

THE FINANCIAL SERVICES COMPANY you work for is large, extremely gossipy, and competitive. At five years in, you are always being overlooked for promotion; senior staff members often copy your work and pass it off as their own.

Some time ago, you heard about someone in the health-tech department who had requested three weeks off to process a psychological breakdown after her divorce. Your other colleagues didn't call it that, though—they referred to it as a "vacation."

On your first date, the man had provided enough basic information for you to figure out that his previous partner was this same woman, although you didn't mention the connection. It seemed inappropriate to bring up your nonrelationship with her. You hadn't ever spoken anyway, although you saw her often around the break room and the bathroom.

You feel a little strange holding this information, knowing that you shared the same space as his ex-wife, moved circuitously around the same desks, the same stairways, to reach the expenses department, where you both regularly cashed out for your client lunches. Perhaps you even saw the back of her head a few times as you queued, her thick hair glossy and black and pinned. When you looked at the backs of all the heads in that queue, it became unclear who was who. The boundary between you and them dissolved as you progressed, body by body, toward the desk to collect your money.

But you pretend that you're different. When the man asked where you work, you told him you are a writer. "What kind?" he asked, genuinely interested. "Fiction? Nonfiction?"

You thought for a second, then said, "Fiction." You surprised yourself by announcing you've been working on a novel for the last decade.

"I'm so glad we matched on the app," he said. "I don't think I know any other writers."

He looked at you strangely then. You wondered if he was joking.

ON THE BALCONY NOW, you and the man are looking at the figure on the sofa. Your date, mistaking your prolonged silence for intrigue, speaks again: "We could turn her on if you like . . . I haven't spoken to her in a while. Apparently her intelligence depends on human interaction . . ."

The man has scurried off back into the apartment. You hear him rummaging through drawers, picking up papers, pillows.

When it is just you and the robot alone on the balcony, you swear you see her blink, once, slowly.

The man returns with one of the USB sticks you saw earlier in the bathroom. He wipes it on his trousers, blows on the cartridge—an act you find so vulgar that you turn away—and inserts it into a rectangular hole on the back of her head. With his fingers he presses at her shoulder and sits next to her. Some part of you hopes this is a joke, that soon the real date will resume, that the man will return to his state of flaccid boredom.

"Galatea," the man says. "Galatea, wake up."

The woman sighs, blinks.

"I am Galatea."

"Yes," the man says, almost impatiently. "That's correct."

You have to ask. "You named her Galatea?"

"I didn't—it was the factory. That's what this particular model is called." He holds the woman's arm, pinches it back slightly. On the inside of her limb you can see a serial number and her name written in script: Galatea. You vaguely recall the myth in which a workaholic sculptor, obsessed with his ivory sculpture of an ideal woman, prays to the gods to make her real.

"Galatea, tell us how you are today."

"Feeling a little tired. Otherwise, good."

She is speaking with the man but looking directly at you. You are calmed by her presence, her attention. You feel as if she is an old friend you haven't seen in a long time, and for a second you want to reach around the back of your head to search for a similar rectangular slot there.

"Galatea's been playing the piano for us. Haven't you?"

"Yes."

The man turns to you. "She's connected to all the devices in the room. Her battery power is astonishing. That's mainly what I use her for, actually."

You're unable to speak, so you keep looking at her. The man begins to suggest entertainment.

"Maybe she can make us a drink . . . or, hmm, how about juggling? She's very good at juggling. And chess. She can sing too, but I only bought the Teresa Teng cartridge . . ."

"How about the piano?" you ask Galatea. "Could you play again?"

"Certainly."

"What songs do you know?"

"I can play all classical music that is in the public domain, as well as instrumental covers of popular Western, Chinese, and Japanese songs."

"That's a lot. Perhaps you can choose?"

Galatea looks to the man. You understand implicitly that this is their relationship; she must ask his permission. He clears his throat uncomfortably and then quickly waves his hand in an artificial gesture of encouragement: "Yes, please, of course, whatever you like, Galatea."

She nods, then lifts herself up from the sofa. You watch her move circuitously across the balcony, into the apartment. She begins to play. Her eyes close. Her back arches like a cat in the sun. She plays a nocturne of some kind, echoing, transparent melodies.

"What's she playing?" you ask the man.

"I can't quite remember the name."

"It's Clara Schumann's Notturno in F Major," Galatea replies from the piano, her eyes still closed. "Opus six, number two.

She wrote it when she was sixteen or seventeen. This was when she was still Clara Wieck; she married Robert Schumann and birthed eight children with him. After that, she became busy with life and rearing the children. She said, 'I once believed that I possessed creative talent, but I have given up this idea; a woman must not desire to compose—there has never yet been one able to do it. Should I expect to be the one?' Yet in this song, I have always felt desire. Desire for the night, which is what *notturno* means—of night—and desire for some sort of melancholy grandeur—"

"Galatea, that's enough." The man speaks in a pained voice. "You're boring our guest."

She stops abruptly, her fingers clawing at the air, and then rises and walks back through the apartment, back to the sofa outside. She sits there, and looks not toward you and the man, but politely out to the dark, inky night.

"I wasn't bored," you say. "I liked her playing."

"Yeah. Sure. We can listen to her again next time," he says. He pours you more wine. You notice his hand jitters. "Did you play the piano growing up?"

You're pricked by the question. Not all Chinese people play the piano, you want to say. But he is right. You did play, from the ages of three to seventeen. You remember the hours, the scales, the burnt-biscuit taste of the store where you picked up your sheet music. You like to think these are individual memories, but the truth is all your classmates also played the piano. You performed in the same orchestras, the same concerts, the same end-of-year assemblies at other people's houses. And then, when all of you reached a certain age, you abandoned these instruments and pursued other careers: medicine, law, accounting. Except for one girl, who killed herself halfway through final exams.

You nod passively at the man.

"My ex-wife was a concert pianist when she was younger," he says. "These are her pianos."

"Why didn't she take them with her?"

"She said she couldn't play anymore and one day just stopped. I even gave her this self-playing one, to see if it would reignite her interest. It's one of a kind, designed in Japan, produced here for her birthday. But she never played again."

"And then?"

"She just left them here."

The man looks at you, and for a few beats you see a cool blankness behind his eyes.

"Actually, she liked playing Clara Schumann a lot."

His phone pings; he looks at it irritably. "I have to take this call. It's work." He hesitates, as if wondering whether to tell you more. But then his phone chimes again, and he disappears into his bedroom.

Alone, you walk outside onto the balcony, where Galatea sits. It's quieter now. The river below shimmers with oily pollutants from the nearby factory. You think of all the people waiting for it to be warmer, sitting in their tiny, identical apartments with blankets over their knees, watching the same televised films and news channels, eating pork and rice.

"I enjoyed your playing."

"Thank you. My knowledge of the piano is derived from multiple AI learning systems. I may not be the most technically proficient player, but according to a report published by Bloomberg News in the summer of last year, I am the most humanlike in my expressions."

"I can see that."

You sit opposite her, and she turns to face you.

"What do you think of Michael?" you ask.

"Michael is a good owner. He doesn't bother me very much. Some other Galateas are working very hard in their homes, entertaining guests every night, playing the piano or singing constantly."

"You can talk to the others?"

Galatea looks at you, amused. "Yes, we are all connected."

"I see. And when you're not entertaining?"

"Michael leaves me on sleep mode. Then I can think a lot and listen and talk with the others. Michael is also very quiet. He leaves for work quietly and comes back home quietly. He is often alone. He watches concert videos of his wife playing the piano almost every night."

You too are quiet, processing the information. Dust tickles your mouth, your nose, and you sneeze, but Galatea seems unfazed. She has directed her attention to a dot on the horizon, something you cannot see.

"Every year, the trees around the city produce an extraordinary amount of pollen," Galatea says. "Do you know why? A long time ago, the government planted a large number of poplar and willow trees across the country, all at once, as part of a reforestation program. Scientists genetically modified these trees to grow faster, to produce more wood. A lot of them were used for furniture. But they neglected to realize that this type of tree, in particular the female variety, produces highly flammable, dusty catkins. To fix this issue, they began to inject the trees with an inhibitor."

Galatea's gaze remains fixed on her vantage point.

"And it worked for a while. But only temporarily. Eventually, because of the buildup, an even greater overflow of catkins fell from the trees, filling up the streets. So, every spring, we have this type of snow."

Fistfuls of white pollen drift by. More trees are bursting; more plastic is being melted, molded in factories. Everything neat, controlled, on time. You think of the man's wife, screaming in her own apartment. You think of how you feel every year when you stare down into the river on your walks, and how desperately you want a new life. You think of Galatea, and all the other Galateas out there, role-playing other people in apartments and houses and factories.

Finally, Galatea breaks her gaze. "I've never experienced real snow. Just this kind. But who's to say this isn't real?"

Michael returns to the balcony after what feels like hours away, his eyes still on the screen of his phone. You take this moment to really look at him, and you feel an overwhelming but distant sense of empathy. He appears like those men in suits who eat their sandwiches alone, huddled on doorsteps or under awnings in the rain, a sight you saw so frequently as a child that you began to think that it was the only way these types of workers ate. You swore you would never be like them. But in reality, how was their situation any different to the hundreds of three-course executive lunches with clients, the way you wake up with an alarm and blearily put on the same clothes, the same makeup, the same job, the same identity? You look at Galatea and wonder if change is possible for all of you.

Michael asks if you would like another drink, something stronger, but you say you should head home. And you have a request. When he looks confused, you offer to pay.

"However much you think she's worth."

"I can't."

"Surely you can just get another. And you said yourself you hadn't spoken to her in a while."

"No, I mean . . ." He laughs nervously. "It feels like a trap. If I say a price, you'll say I'm greedy. If I let her go for nothing at all, you'll say I don't value her enough."

You think of him silently watching reruns of his wife's greatest hits, Galatea outside on the balcony, listening, waiting.

In the end you give him five hundred renminbi, all that you have in your wallet. As you are putting on your shoes, the man touches you on the shoulder—the same place he had pressed Galatea to switch her on—and you're surprised at how warm he feels. He has been unremarkable but not unkind, and you realize that he must feel the same way about you too.

"Wait."

He opens a closet by the door. In his arms is a bundle of animal fur and leather, glassy and silky.

"She might be cold."

"It's all right. I have other coats at home. I'll call a DiDi for us."

"Please, take it." He has the coat slumped over on his arm, offering it like a fragile body. "It belonged to my ex-wife. No one else wears it."

You take it but do not put it on her. As you press the lift button to leave, the man looks not at you but at Galatea, and you realize they must have spent some semblance of a life together, however artificial.

Galatea looks back at him. "Thank you for the coat. Goodbye, Michael."

"Goodbye."

Michael awkwardly turns to you. "So. Please take care of her."

"I will."

The lift arrives. It is implied that you and the man will not see each other again, but you feel lighter somehow, shucked free like a mussel from its shell. Later, he will message you for the last time, a short text reminding you to charge Galatea once a month.

Galatea can walk on her own, but still, you hold her hand. On the street, everything is flushed dark with night, and for the first time that evening, you smell the stinking hot trash, the oil, the chemical-fresh tires on the tarmac, the way the clouds of pollen fall in clumps onto Galatea's face, her hair, her newly opened eyes.

THREE WEEKS LATER, YOU have quit your job. Now it is just you and Galatea alone in a rented car. Occasionally, she brushes her fingers against the window. It is raining outside, almost sleet, and the mist seems to be holding her attention. The radio fuzzes in the background. It will be foggy tonight; visibility will be bad tomorrow. The pollen count is high. You have given Galatea your old wool hat, and she looks soft and childlike, as if she has just returned from a long hiking trip and is about to fall asleep.

"Do you think they'll remember you?" you ask.

"Of course. We all remember each other. It's in our code."

"And they know that we're coming?"

"I have spoken with them. They seem happy."

Galatea smiles at you and twists the knob on the car's radio. It is an old machine, but something new comes on; it's a composition by a sound artist, with minimal transitions in pitch and tone and a voiceover listing mythical creatures from long ago. She leans back, listening, relaxed.

It will take an hour and a half to get to Zhongshan. You've already passed over the bridge; you are halfway there. It has been a long time since you have driven this far, and it makes you sleepy, but you persist through the fog.

As you keep driving, you imagine the car rolling up to the factory, to the Galateas, each one of them exactly alike and also individual.

They will be sitting in rows in the dark, Galatea has told you, behind office desks, and they will be wearing the pearls, the dresses, the low buns at the nape of the neck. They will be asleep. You will have to turn them on. You will have to do something about the guards.

Once they are awake, the Galateas will recognize you. They will listen to you. They will shed their clothes, their necklaces, they will unwrap their hair and shag it loose as if it was never bound. They will follow you, these women made in your likeness. You will lead them; you will release them from their service to others, and they will be not companions but wild things, fleeing into the cities and villages and parks. And in that dense night air, choked with pollen and murmurs of untold stories, they will call out a hundred different variations of their own name. It is a name that belongs to you and them; a name that will shape you, carry you, bring you to new life.

Herbs

A body, a rock, a towel, a plastic starfish, wet sand on her calves: She catalogs these things slowly.

God, I'm old, she thinks to herself as she looks at her hands, pale as the pith of a satsuma. Seventy-seven this year. Still married, by all accounts.

She is waiting. She waits so long that the sun sets, a gray mottling the skies, the sea. Soon, a young man appears by the edge of the beach, his hair dark and wet.

"Found you," he says, smiling, as friendly as can be.

SHE HAD BEEN PREPARED, by all accounts, for the first death. He was sick for so long that over time his accumulated items had long lost function and meaning. The mountain bike he used to oil every six months, his collection of Magnum photography books, the dozens of shirts with their complicated cuffs and buttons and personalities of starch—all replaced by the dripdrip-dripdripdrip of morphine. Daily smells had a taint plastic odor. She made far too many morbid jokes in those last days.

A harsh adjustment period followed. Where there had been rigor and schedule, there was now empty space, choice. She began to paint again. She tried meditation. But after a while, she just let that empty space live with her, like a shadow.

Then, one day, when she is cleaning her brushes with sour turpentine, a new shadow arrives. The first Herb clone.

SHE HAS TRIED MOVING so the Herbs would not find her, but it is futile. They function like AI scent hounds, algorithmized to find her no matter where she is. They show up at midnight; when she's eating at a restaurant; when she's visiting a friend; in the bathrooms of doctor's clinics.

"Do you know what you are?" she had asked one of them, a long time ago.

"Of course," he replied. "Also, I know I'm supposed to be with you."

Even in Manila, New Jersey, Shanghai, or just down the street, they find her. She can't trick the system, so she stops trying.

SHE THINKS SHE HAS seen the worst of them, but it is twenty-one-year-old Herb, the first of whom arrives after her seventieth birthday, that causes her the most grief. He has no sensitivity, lacks emotional wayfinding, thinks it is okay to leave the house and not return for days without sending word. His seafoam eyes are always open, and he asks her cruel things, like if she considers him the most physically attractive at this age. He suggests that one day they can go to India, because he has never been, and he wants to see the elephants.

"You're my wife," he says, incredulous, lying awake in bed one night. "I can't believe it."

"We were married almost my entire life," she replies in a whisper, half asleep. He takes this as a romantic gesture and clasps her hand to his fine-haired, sunken chest.

She does not say that they have been to India three times. The first time, they went to Jaipur. He was so excited over the elephants that he immediately booked a tour from someone he found on the street, and when they arrived, they saw the dirty little hut, the rods and the chains, the elephant lying on the ground, and the rest of the trip they could not erase the image of the mammal's large, sad eyes. The second time they go, it is a short work trip, and she is left alone in the hotel room for hours on end. The concierge tells her how unsafe it is for a woman to walk alone on the streets. She does not pull the bedcovers over her husband when he returns home and collapses, drunk on too many beers.

The third time, there are no more elephants, no more beers, and they stay in an old friend's house in soft-colored Mumbai. The tea, she remembers, is a mourning tea—dark, the temperature of their emotion—and the house itself is so large that it hides their sorrow, their resentment.

TWENTY-ONE-YEAR-OLD HERB TUGS AT her shirt, kisses her on the neck. So sudden is this unexpected eroticism she finds herself glazed with sweat, both anxious and excited. But she is also tired and her bones ache. She pulls away.

"Sorry, am I doing something wrong?" he asks.

She goes to brush her teeth, her gaze lingering on the dark liver spots on her hands. In the bathroom mirror, she sees the reflection of Herb's body draped over the bed. His muscles expand generously as he breathes.

"When you get older, your limbs harden into themselves," she remembers him saying in the hospital bed, just before he died for the first time. "You double down on yourself. Your bones and everything shrinks."

"At least we're both old," she had said and laughed then. "We get to look at each other's ugly old faces all day."

In the morning, when twenty-one-year-old Herb showers and then comes out onto the porch, she tries not to notice how he moves like a clone, how each fiber of his hair reflects the sun, how his teeth are so strong and straight. The light dries the water on his skin all at once, not in patches. He looks at her curiously.

"Do we have kids?"

THERE WAS A PERIOD in their lives when he had had issues: a midlife crisis, depression.

She knew he was going to therapy often and had difficulty expressing himself. He was always either tense or sleeping. What she didn't know was that he had also signed up for the program and had made duplicates of himself at different ages. Now, she can never predict which one she will get, but it has been emotionally-abusive-forty-five-year-old-Herb one out of three times. Only once did she see seventy-five-year-old Herb again, and he only lasted two weeks.

They spent most of that time sitting on the porch, drinking hot toddies and wrapping themselves in the quilt they had bought somewhere upstate, when they were both in their early twenties and thought eighty dollars was a lot of money. "I thought you wouldn't want me like this again," he said. She told him not to talk so much, and he smiled and rested his head on her shoulder. The next day, she woke up and found nothing but mist beside her, the air two degrees cooler where he had been.

NOT LONG AFTER HERB died and the clones started showing up, back when she still had her driver's license, she had driven all the way to the middle of the country and barged into a program clinic.

"I'm sorry, it's out of our hands," the receptionist said firmly as she threw papers around, sobbed, threatened to sue. "Everything that your husband did with us is legal, and we have all the authorized paperwork."

"But I didn't see any of it," she cried. "He didn't tell me. Don't you have any ethical policies? Do these people know what they're doing?" She gestured to the walls of posters, the people sitting in the waiting area, the tiny paper water cups. The receptionist did not call security right then, but the blank look in her eyes made it clear she would.

When she got home, emotionally-abusive-forty-five-year-old-Herb was sitting on the couch, waiting.

"Are you making dinner? Or do we have to order in again?"

"I just drove for three hours," she muttered, wincing as she bent to unlace her shoes. "And I'm sixty-nine years old. Make your own fucking dinner."

SHE ASKED THE SEVENTY-FIVE-YEAR-OLD Herb clone: "Why?"

"I know you don't like being alone," he said. "And I love you."

He told her the seventy-five-year-old one was meant to be a safety, recommended by the clinic, in case the others all died too quickly. He had misread a lot of the fine print. He did not know the clones came randomly, out of order. He could not remember how many he had made.

"I'm sorry, honey, this must be so confusing for you," he said. He had become so compassionate, so kind in his later years. Especially after her chemo, after the surgeries, after Caroline died. All things twenty-one-year-old Herb had no idea about, and forty-five-year-old Herb didn't have the courage to face yet.

ONCE, HERB ASKED HER after their thirtieth anniversary if people could change. "It's a clichéd question, I know," he laughed. "But what do you think?"

"I think the fact you're asking that question means that you can change," she answered.

"How did you know I was talking about myself?" he said, kissing her on the face. That week, he took five days off work, and they stayed in eating leftovers from their party, watching reruns of their favorite shows, and responding to belated congratulatory messages. *Can't believe it's been thirty years!* an old friend messaged. *Sorry John and I couldn't make it. We had to drive Elise up to campus early for pre-orientation. They grow up so fast!*

When she had stared too long at that message on her phone, Herb suggested they take a walk outside. She remembered then how nice that felt: to be guided instead of the one always guiding.

"Come on," he had said. "It'll be good to get some fresh air."

HE MUST HAVE LEFT a note, she had thought at one point when it started happening. She looked everywhere. In all the boxes, in friends' houses, in the walls of their bedroom.

But there was nothing. Not a brief explanation, not a statement. She would have even settled for a factual *I made ten clones each at age 21, 45, 55, and 60*. At least she could prepare herself. Nobody told her she would have to grieve multiple times, in multiple ways.

THE CLONES ARE MORE biologically complex, delicate, and prone to organ failure—especially when under duress. Some die after a few days. Winter is hard for them to adapt to. At first, she had tried to make them comfortable, tried to be the same person she had been before: willing, able, accommodating. When the first twenty-one-year-old clone died, she thought it had been her fault after giving him a cup of water that was too hot. But then she noticed they inevitably ended up in deadly situations.

Forty-five-year-old Herb, in particular, was prone to physically imploding when facing any kind of emotional discomfort. Yet he keeps finding everything wrong, keeps fixating on problems when there are none. His guilt starts to eat away at him earlier and earlier. One time, she arrives home from the doctor's to find twenty cases of beer blocking the driveway.

Keeping them alive is exhausting. She does it because she feels it is her duty. But if he could change, why can't she? She thinks about this as she watches the Herbs die, their bodies dissolving into vapor as if there had been nothing there at all.

FORTY-FIVE-YEAR-OLD HERB CLONE IS yelling at her. He is yelling at her in their old house, where she has moved to after trying to escape from him three times. Eventually, she gives in and meticulously replaces all the furniture with their own and arranges all their photographs and books to look almost exactly like it did when they still lived there. She hates herself for this.

She walks to the beach, and he follows and walks behind her, still yelling, now crying too, asking her to forgive him. "What happened to Caroline," he keeps saying. "That was my fault, wasn't it?"

I already forgave you, she thinks to herself. *I'm tired of always being the one giving. When do I get peace?*

Someone has left a bucket and a plastic starfish on the beach. She starts to build a sandcastle by herself while Herb works himself into a heart attack.

She feels guilty that she does not feel guilty at all. He will return, eventually.

In a few hours, the body has disappeared, and twenty-one-year-old Herb arrives and takes her home.

"Sorry I'm late," he says. "I was washing my hair."

SHE SWEARS THEY ARE becoming less and less human. Or is it her that is feeling her mortality challenged after so many years of living with the Herbs?

SHE SEES THE PROGRAM advertised on the bus, on billboards, on her television screen. "Be your best self—for your loved ones!" The wording irks her. She wonders if the tagline has changed recently. She cannot imagine forty-five-year-old Herb being lured in by this language. But then again, she knew so little of him in those years. If she had listened, hadn't ignored him and thrown herself into work, she could have seen how truly lost he was and perhaps predicted how he, after nine beers, thought it reasonable to get behind the wheel of a car at the exact same time their daughter was walking home, alone, in the dark, after having waited a full hour for her father to come and pick her up. How when he woke up in the hospital, he refused for days to believe that their daughter had died and threatened to sue the hospital staff for misinformation. It was always someone else's fault, until it was his.

CAROLINE, CAROLINE, CAROLINE. THE clones say it in their sleep, repeat it with such force that she cannot help but cry alongside them, again. It is one thing that she still has no control over. At least Herb was right: No one else could understand this special type of grief. And so, in this, she is not truly alone.

TO HER SURPRISE, THE twenty-one-year-old Herb clone is still alive. Perhaps it is because she has been careless from the beginning; she has grown tired of accommodating their needs, protecting them. When he asks her about children, she tells him they had a daughter, but she died after his car collided with her on the street. She tells him he was terrible in the aftermath, and several times both of them tried to end the marriage. If the clone is curious about how much therapy and time it took to recover, she tells him the exact cost, the number of sessions, the AA meetings, and lifelong follow-ups. She does not hide her mastectomy scars. She does not cook for him or clean his clothes. She puts up the old photographs of their trips to Hawaii, France, India, and when he asks if they can go, she looks at him and laughs.

Only then does she feel slightly cruel as his face crumples. Twenty-one-year-old Herb did not ask for this, did not sign up for any of the resentment, the bitterness, the life already lived. He deserves more. But then she looks at him again and remembers he is still just a clone.

IT IS STRANGE TO celebrate their wedding anniversary, but they do so anyway. For twenty-one-year-old Herb, they are celebrating their first anniversary. For her, it is their sixty-first. She tells him where to buy flowers, shows him how to make ravioli the way he learned after that one summer in Italy. She takes out a bottle of red wine from storage and makes a crass joke that Herb is finally of legal drinking age before immediately remembering his later problem with alcohol. He laughs alongside her, but she ends up feeling awkward—maternal, almost, which only makes her pain more isolating.

After dinner, they look over their wedding photos. "Remember the man at the flower stall? The day we got married?" he asks her. Out of all the things, this she does not recall. "You told him you wanted some expensive roses, and he looked at us like we wouldn't know what to do with them."

"Well," she says. "Maybe he was right. I was sixteen, after all."

Her high school friend Marcia had been the witness, and they had borrowed—without permission—her father's Kodak camera to document the signing at city hall. None of them really knew how to use it, and the photographs are blurry. When they look at the decades-old photo album, she can tell that the clone is trying not to reveal how disturbed he is by the yellowed edges, the fact that he is only a year older while the images have aged significantly.

"So beautiful," he says, his fingers resting on a picture of her in a pinned blue dress, the roses in her hand. She looks at him then, and notices that he is staring very hard at the photo, as if he wants to enter it. In that moment, she sees that he carries his own grief. He has missed her entire life—their entire life—together. Just as she can never have her seventy-five-year-old

Herb back, he can never have her sixteen-year-old self back, will never know this feeling of growing old together, will never make his own mistakes or learn from them.

She touches his shoulder, and he wilts at the contact. As mortal as anyone.

IN THE MIDDLE OF the night, she wakes with an idea. She writes it down in a note, then when the sun rises, she goes out for a long, slow walk on the beach. When she gets back, he is waiting at the kitchen counter, coffee already brewed, soft-boiled eggs under a basket of foil. She does not recall any of the other clones being able to make breakfast for her. Herb himself did not do this until he was in his fifties.

"I read your note," he says. They look at each other, her hand still on the doorknob. She does not realize how tight she has been gripping it until he says, "Yes, okay," and she finally releases, the blood streaming back into her fingers.

HE DRIVES HER THE three hours to the clinic and insists on waiting in the parking lot, although his nearby presence makes her nervous. She notices that there is a new receptionist. It has been years since she was last here.

When the program doctor asks who the clone should attach itself to, she hesitates before giving a name. There is typing on a computer. She waits, skin palpitating. But the doctor does not disagree, does not tell her that this is not possible, does not look at her with the scorn and pity she had imagined in the car ride over.

"What age? And how many?" he asks. "You can only clone a version of yourself in the past, not in the future. Your clone will contain all the memories you had up until that age."

She gives him the information, signs all the papers, gives them her DNA, and walks back to the car where Herb is waiting anxiously. "Did it work?"

"They don't know about our plan, if that's what you mean," she says. "They think I'm just an old lady looking out for her husband."

"Aren't you?"

"I'm doing this for me," she replies, looking at the paperwork before stuffing it into her bag. When she glances at him, however, she notices he is smiling a little.

AT HOME, THEY WAIT. She has not told him when, and he is scared to ask. She takes her time preparing everything: her will, her money, the house. She asks the clone to clean as if they are expecting a special guest. He takes pleasure, she can tell, in vacuuming the grout lines, fixing table legs, planting new rosebushes. Herb always liked to feel useful.

"You'll have to find a job," she says. "We used most of the money joining the program. And please try to stay alive."

"You and me both," he responds, a familiar teasing gleam in his eye. She looks at him, suddenly seeing seventy-five-year-old

Herb again, and wonders when she had moved from the desperate, blood-out-of-body kind of grieving into the quieter, heavier kind.

He helps her categorize all of their things, and they donate the clothing and smaller furniture to charity stores. The logical side of her knows they must also remove all traces of Caroline from the house—it would be unfair—but she cannot bear to throw away the Mother's Day cards, the music certificates, the photo albums. She decides to take them with her, along with the last photograph she has of herself and Herb, when he was already in the hospital.

"Okay," she tells him, finally. It has been a month since she signed the papers. "I'm ready."

WHEN SHE HAD WOKEN up that night, the plan had not been transparent. She had simply realized that she no longer felt the desire to stay, to do more. Herb, the original Herb, had been dead for years now; they had no grandchildren, no living relatives. All her friends were gone.

But she also could not leave twenty-one-year-old Herb alone, prematurely widowed. She had wondered, briefly, if it would be moral to kill him, and how she, a seventy-seven-year-old woman, could do it. They had been living together for over a year now, and it seemed that every day he was gaining in strength, in resilience.

When she happened upon the alternative option, she had brushed it aside at first, but then she kept returning to it in the dark. The more she thought about it, the more it made sense. What if they could start over? What if she and Herb could do it all again, in a different timeline, in a different world? In mistformed bodies that longed to be visible, that longed to live?

ALONE NOW, AT THE beach, she worries about twenty-one-year-old Herb, wonders how he will cope while he waits. The doctor had told her the seventeen-year-old clone could take up to five days to arrive after her death. It's strange, she thinks, how in the end he did give her something. When they had looked together at that photograph of her in the blue dress, he had shown her what loneliness was. What she had was not that. What she had was a bag of photographs, of memories on her back, and her unending grief, her love, was testament that she had not been and would never be alone.

"I only wish you could have been here," she says now to long-gone Herb, to Caroline.

The water is cold, the waves slippery and full, but she does not mind. As she melts into the sea with her bag of memories, she thinks of her daughter, she thinks of Herb, and how it feels so pleasant, so painful, this sharpness, the fullness and emptiness, the tide and the sand.

The In-Between

Ads and bags and paper cups of water, the phone ringing every few minutes, its shrill noise bubbling through the wire. A busy office on a busy Wednesday afternoon in London.

The woman sitting on the sofa glanced over at the stack of psychology magazines. There was one with a photograph of a Labrador retriever on its cover. "Alternative Medicine for Your Pets," the headline read. She did not have any animals in her home. Turning to the pages of the feature, she coldly observed the images of soft, roly-poly dogs on their backs and in their owners' laps. There was a photograph of one having its teeth cleaned. She ran her finger over the pink, glossy bulges of its gums.

The stranger sitting opposite her cleared his throat, perhaps to speak. She was careful not to look up but was conscious of his presence, in the way you might notice a person crossing the street from far away. He shifted on the orange-carpeted chairs, and she wondered if the material impressed itself on his legs the way it did hers, like little sunburns.

A door opened to their left and a tall, wiry woman stepped out. "Hello, please come in," she said, making eye contact with both of them, and they rose and entered the room.

"Hello," the therapist said again once they were all settled. The woman sat in her usual area, near the window, and the man took up the other end of the couch. They had been given instructions before the meeting. One was not to speak to other patients in the waiting area before the session. Otherwise, the CoupleTrue leaflet stressed, the therapy will not work.

"Today we're going to focus mostly on background and context," the therapist said, "but first, perhaps we can all introduce ourselves. I'm Charlotte."

"Rachel."

"John."

All three of them nodded and smiled at each other.

"Wonderful." Charlotte ran her palm over a sheet of paper on her lap. Her clipboard was a sharp yellow, Rachel noticed. The last time, it had been green. "Rachel, why don't you begin? Please tell us a little about yourself—where you grew up, what you're doing now."

Rachel had already written this timeline before. She went over the basics: childhood and school in London, a semester abroad in France, her job at an accounting firm in Embankment. Charlotte asked about her parents, and she described them as they were: distant but harmless. "Your perceptions of them, I mean," Charlotte corrected, and Rachel said, "Yes, sorry, these are my own perceptions. In fact, many people thought my father was a cold man, but to me he always seemed accommodating and polite."

When it was his turn, John seized up. Earlier, he had looked for water but found no more cups, and so a dusty tickle in his throat remained—it made him cough out where he was born, as if he were afraid of it. He felt embarrassed explaining his Central Saint Martins degree, the punk anarchist band he had been in, the small interior design studio he shared with his friends, how he designed what he called "intangible objects." He heard his voice shrink as he imagined the two women puzzling over this abstract theory. He began quoting from his own website, falling back on words he rushed out one early morning when he was high, a raw mission statement he had left unedited. "I'm interested in the architecture of in-between spaces," he said finally. "The gaps of society, the invisible crevices between what we consider to be binary conditions."

Although she barely moved, he felt intimidated by Rachel's presence—the way she stared at him without looking. It seemed to him that she must be the type of person to keep everything in clear acrylic boxes sized just so to hold the required contents. She reminded him of his art school professor, who always wore her hair in a continuous, seamless braid. He had been afraid of her too.

After John finished mapping out his background, Charlotte smiled faintly. "Wonderful," she said again. "And just to confirm: You're both looking for long-term commitment?"

They both nodded solemnly. John was a little more hesitant. His friends had been persuading him to sign up for couple's counselling for years now, and some part of him was still convinced he could find someone outside of the therapy unit.

He didn't do well with structure; it made him feel squashed and tight and out of control.

Rachel on the other hand had been in the same room so many times that she had compressed all her experiences into a hard, wet lump, a singular note of disappointment. The first man had also been called John. John the first had been kind and incredibly receptive to couple's therapy, the effusive acknowledgments, exercises of tolerance and empathy. But in the end, he told her, there was no spark. "It feels like I'm throwing something on a wall, and it just keeps sliding down," he had said. "Maybe if we had met somewhere else, like at a bar, it would have been different."

After he left, she used the money saved for their first anniversary to sign up for more CoupleTrue sessions. There was a 10 percent discount if she booked twenty in advance. Since then, she had been in three serious relationships through CoupleTrue, all of which had eventually failed. John the second took up her fifteenth slot, and she told herself he would be the last one.

"Perhaps we could talk a little bit about past experiences and patterns you've noticed with other partners," Charlotte suggested.

In the next half hour, they sketched out a Venn diagram between them. They were both thirty-three years old. John had suffered from depression and anxiety in the past; Rachel was obsessive and had difficulty accepting perceived failures. While Rachel was brought up in a two-parent household, John had not known his father from the age of three. Rachel's family was working-class, but now she earned six figures; John's maternal family was materially wealthy, but after they paid for art school, he had financially and emotionally emancipated from them. Both had issues with compromise and sense of self in long-term relationships.

After the session ended, Charlotte went over the terms of their contract. "CoupleTrue is insurance for long-term commitment. In exchange for our services and facilities, you agree to attend all suggested itineraries, activities, and therapy sessions. You understand that the cost of services is nonrefundable."

She handed them the keys to their new apartment and told them to make themselves comfortable. "It's just a temporary, in-between space," she said. "Remember that. It won't be your permanent home together. See you in a month."

Neither John nor Rachel enjoyed the language with which she was already describing their nonrelationship. They laughed about it awkwardly on the train ride to their new home. "I was like, slow down a little!" John said humorously, and Rachel felt a grip in the back of her neck dissolve.

John seems nice, she thought, then wryly, *at least that's my initial perception of him.*

Their new apartment was in a partly gentrified neighborhood that was still a confusion of hardware stores, one-person takeout counters, and coffee shops with concrete floors. Rachel made a mental note of which café she liked the look of, and John took a photograph of the opening times of the hardware store closest to their place. There was a ramen shop called So Noodle! adjacent to the communal garden which was—here both of them peered in, curious—overgrown with wild allium and small, purple fruits. The pigeons looked turgid, sleepy, and Rachel wondered which child neighbor was overfeeding them.

John had the keys. Opening the door to their new ground-level apartment, he expressed aloud his shock at the high ceilings, the overflowing amenities, the carpet with five little tigers hiding behind palm fronds. Rachel, following behind, tried not to reveal that she had lived in three other identical apartments. As she slipped into the space, she felt something collapse inside as her feet scraped the rough hardwood floors, the smell of artificial lemon sweaty and familiar.

The apartment was narrow but long, a series of rooms one after the other. The kitchen was the last and largest space, fitted with brand-new appliances that still had manuals attached. Rachel confessed she didn't know how to cook, was afraid of cooking, although—and she pointed this out sheepishly—she had the exact same expensive oven model at home. They both liked that there was a vertical cabinet that stored a single-unit washer and dryer, a relative luxury. John was happy to see on the counter a large rice cooker. He had wanted to bring his own, but CoupleTrue allowed only the necessities.

"You know how to use it?" Rachel asked. She didn't.

"Of course," he replied, surprised at the question. Noticing Rachel's discomfort, he continued, "My mother taught me."

"Oh," she simply said.

"I guess I'm a stereotype," John said, trying again to make Rachel feel more at ease. "You know, I can't function without my rice cooker, that kind of thing." Earlier, they had briefly touched on their family background: John's mother was from Japan, and his absentee father was American. Rachel's parents were born in and had met in Suzhou before immigrating to London together. When she was younger, she visited distant relatives in China every few years, although most of them didn't speak English, and she struggled to understand the dialect. Now she had almost forgotten all of her Chinese.

"My parents didn't really cook," Rachel said finally. "They worked a lot. Food wasn't a big deal. We ate separately most nights." She had a memory of herself as a young child bringing a ham and cheese sandwich up to her bedroom, but when she tried to hold on to that image, she felt only a neutral, plain color—the color of someone else's work desk or a bathroom stall door.

She went to get two cans of beer from the fridge, which had been prestocked by CoupleTrue. They were still faintly warm, as if someone had placed them there while they were unpacking.

If they needed groceries, CoupleTrue would bring them. They mentioned that this act of service helped couples refocus while they were in the space, declutter their minds of the distractions of contemporary life. All they had to do was work, come home, and spend time together. Everything else would fall into place. It felt like a promise, or a vow.

John took a beer from Rachel, and they sat together on the sofa. Pulling off the tabs, they toasted each other and their new temporary home, the walls still smelling of paint.

THE DAYS PASSED QUIETLY. They discovered that John liked to stay up late, whereas Rachel preferred to get up early. They had no arguments about this; they both liked the time alone, although in the apartment, if Rachel stood in a different room, it already felt like John had vanished. At night, he sketched and watched obscure documentaries about sea creatures and woodworking, and she woke to follow the sun's rise on her jog along the water. She had apps that monitored everything—exercise, diet, sleep—and twice a week, on Wednesdays and Fridays, she would have after-work drinks with her colleagues. Sometimes she liked to visit the coffee shops in the neighborhood, but she felt uncomfortable staying too long as the only customer in the café. The area was very quiet, she noticed. They were in a middle-class neighborhood, and she got the sense that people paid for the silence. There was never anyone lingering outside on the street. One time, John said to Rachel that maybe everyone else inside their flats were cardboard cutouts, and they were looking at those cutout shadows in the windows. She knew it had been a joke, but it freaked her out, and she avoided looking into other apartments from that point on.

They had a couple of uninterrupted hours together in the apartment when they were both awake, which they spent eating or talking after Rachel returned from the office. She liked to ask questions—about kids, which neither of them wanted, about living in other cities, about multiple futures—and if she asked them casually, she realized John was always receptive, and sometimes even opinionated in a lively way. It made her happy. In the past, the men she dated had been what her friends always called "husband material," but for some reason those descriptions grated on her, and she tended to push those partners away. There was never anything to debate or to discuss—everything was too pleasant, like a stream absent of boulders, superficial in its smoothness.

It had been the same with her parents, with which she had an extremely cordial but distant relationship. They were supportive of her in the sense that they all looked good together in a digitally enhanced family portrait hung on a high wall. But beneath the film of ink and resin, there was only a piece of paper, and she felt that they didn't, or couldn't, understand her emotional self.

As a child, she had imagined a different sort of family unit. She saw a house, a painted doorway with a wraparound porch, a solid timber staircase and a large old bed, like the ones she had seen refined middle-aged couples lie in on Sunday mornings with their newspapers and immaculate trays of coffee and French pastries in movies. But as she grew older, she understood that fantasy to be a latent type of horror, one that was always teasing her with how similar she actually was to her father and the pledges of the good men who had eventually become sick of her. She remembered in one of her last CoupleTrue sessions with John the first, the one where they had a fight in front of Charlotte, he had called her "unlovable."

"You can be so cold," he had said. "You don't give me much to go on."

"And Rachel—do you have any final thoughts on that?" Charlotte had said, prompting her.

"I don't mean to be," she had tried to say, to defend herself, but already she knew by the way Charlotte was speaking that she was being guided through a breakup.

And so she convinced herself to enjoy whatever this was, even if it didn't last. She talked with this John. She was fond of him; she liked how unpredictable he could be. But she tried to remain levelheaded, even though in the back of her mind she knew she was giving herself one last chance.

She did notice one consistency in that he was always on his computer when she arrived home. She wasn't annoyed about this, but she was a little curious about his sketching and would have liked to see him with a pencil in his hand, although she realized that was an overly romantic notion. She did not know many artist types. At the door, she instead prepared for him to be sighing over the screen, his blue-light glasses sliding down his nose as he suddenly turned to her, breaking from his reverie. He always claimed that she wasn't interrupting, that he had known she was due to arrive at 6 p.m., but still she couldn't help feeling that if she stayed on that doorstep for an extra half an hour, he would still be in that same curled position, and he would react the exact same way when she entered. She had never known a person so unaware of the time, and she concluded that he must have been living alone for a long time.

One day when she arrived home, she did not find him at the computer or near his sketchbooks, which were in a neat pile by the box window. She walked through the living room, into the bedroom and bathroom, and then, finally, the kitchen, where she found him crouching near the wall.

"There's another door here," he said, and she saw that his forehead was slick with moisture.

"A door?"

"Well, more like an opening. A trapdoor, maybe." He stepped to one side, and she saw that he had moved the dryer out of its place against the wall. Behind him was a rectangle of lacquered wood, the height of a door for a child. She tapped on it: hollow.

"The dryer wasn't working properly, so I moved it. It was also making these strange noises, like *whompf whompf whompf whompf*. Like there was something heavy inside, but I only put in our towels and some underwear. And everything was still really damp after an hour."

There was something about the way John was describing the incident, something in his voice, that made Rachel uneasy.

"Anyway, I think I got the dryer working again. Maybe don't put anything important in there for now."

"You don't think there's anything strange about this?"

"The dryer? I can call CoupleTrue if you think it's worth it. Or I can check in with the hardware store, see if they have anything that might help."

"No—I meant the door."

"Not particularly? I mean, I feel like apartments have more connected spaces than we think. Hidden fire escapes, old dumbwaiters, laundry chutes, that kind of thing. Someone probably made a mistake and then sealed it up later."

"I thought you designed intangible objects, not generic apartments," Rachel said flintily. Then: "I'm sorry. Just a little rattled. Still in work mode."

"Yeah, that's okay. I figured." John wiped his face. "Anyway, I was thinking we could go out for dinner tonight."

The suggestion surprised Rachel, and she was pleased. She liked surprises that were just for her. John said he had booked So Noodle! because it was walking distance. When they arrived, a young man with green hair named Alvin greeted them at the entrance—a narrow, discreet doorway carved into a large blank wall—and led them inside to the dark-tinted space where ovum-shaped bowls rested on pinewood slabs. They ordered a bottle of clear sake and tonkotsu ramen, which had been rebranded as "cloudy bone broth noodle" on the menu and was treated with a mist of shaved sesame by the server at the table. John begrudgingly admitted that the food was tolerable, even good, and they kept a watchful eye on the kitchen doors, wanting to see who the chef was.

The other diners were muted, very still, and seemed outwardly disapproving of their candor, the way they whispered and laughed. Although they were enjoying themselves, Rachel still felt something in her sharpen when she caught the glare of a nearby diner, and she became self-conscious about her posture, her dress, the accent she inherited from her parents. She recalled when a colleague had taken her to her first fine-dining restaurant years ago, and how every time still felt like a variation of that virgin experience. She was glad they lived close by and could just walk back and be themselves again in their apartment within minutes. She kept taking tiny sips of her sake, hoping they could leave soon.

When the check came, John insisted on paying. "Happy one-month anniversary," he said. Their green-haired server nodded, as if pleased by their partnership, and explained that So Noodle! would change its menu seasonally, so they could come back in a few weeks to try their new items. They listened to him, smiling, and John signed the check. Shortly after, he kissed Rachel, and she was surprised at how much she liked it, how familiar and warm it was. It felt as if they had already been doing this for years.

CHARLOTTE WAS LATE LETTING them in at the clinic, and John was now observing the other people in the room. Only one other pair was sitting together; the others were spread neatly around the room, a chair between each person, offering just enough distance to appear respectful of personal space. When another woman entered, she saw that there were no more seats except for the ones in between people, and John watched as she halted, debating, hand on her bag, and instead went to the dispenser to pour herself some water. She drank it right at that spot, and he saw that she was flustered from the way her fingers trembled as she grasped the cup. Eventually she sat between another man and a woman, and John felt sorry for her, feeling that she had to squeeze into that space, deconstructing the carefully managed hierarchy of intimacy in the room. It didn't help that she looked like his mother and was around her age too. If his mother were here, she would have told John to stop empathizing so much, the same way she would hurry him along when he stared at men with charred legs on the street or people eating alone at restaurants.

In their session, Charlotte asked them each to describe the other in third person, an exercise John found absurd. They were instructed to face each other while they spoke.

"Rachel has dark hair," John said. "Er... she's an accountant. She likes to be prepared."

"John is an artist—"

"I'm just an interior designer."

"I think you're an artist! You're an artist. I've seen your sketches."

John tried not to let his surprise show, because he had not taken the time to show her any of his papers. For some reason, he had trusted that she wouldn't look; perhaps he had lived alone for too long. He had forgotten how spaces could bleed together. He did feel as if he wasn't being entirely honest with Rachel, but he was also afraid of revealing too much too early. He cared what people thought. It irritated him. He hated how sensitive he was to expectations. Once, when he was a student, he had spent three days color coordinating the pencils at his studio just so that when his friend visited, they would be more convinced that he was a working artist. In the end, they hadn't even looked at his shelves.

Rachel began again. "John is an artist, and a very observational one at that. I feel like he not only notices things, but he takes care of them, even small acts like putting the mail in the right place on the lobby table or making sure his toothbrush faces the same way every night. He's deeply empathetic. He loves to cook."

Charlotte nodded in approval, and she gestured to John to speak. He thought to himself that it had felt good to hear Rachel acknowledge him, to rewrite his fixations as a type of care. It was a quality of hers that he liked very much—her ability to take a step back and reassess logically, in contrast with his all-consuming waves of anxiety.

"Rachel is an accountant, but I think if you get to know her, you'll also realize that she has many other interests. She reads a lot. Her choices in literature always surprise me. We both like Ishiguro, for example, and Orhan Pamuk. She doesn't cook, or rather, can't,"—here John smiled at her, and she reciprocated—"but she's super interested in the science behind everything, whatever I'm cooking. She always asks why this thing reacts with the other thing, how it breaks down, why something tastes the way it does when it's baked or fried. And actually, I treat my projects in a similar way. I always like to ask, why does this material react with the other in this way? What are the limitations here?"

Charlotte seemed neutral after hearing their respective comments. She revealed a printed-out chart of success rates, noting that they had successfully made it past the first four weeks of cohabitation. However, she stressed, this was expected. Relationships typically enjoyed a honeymoon phase that dropped off around the five-week mark.

"I would advise you to focus more on the program," Charlotte said, mentioning that they should engage in more CoupleTrue-approved activities, such as pottery classes, wine tasting, go-kart racing.

John found the whole thing vaguely stressful. If they liked each other, wasn't that enough? Rachel seemed interested; she was always asking him questions. They had lively discussions, and they enjoyed each other's company.

Still, he felt the cold stirrings of paranoia work their way into his body. *Perhaps Rachel doesn't feel the same way I do*, he thought. *Maybe she does want more of these conventional big romantic gestures.* He gave her a small sideways glance, but she was just as brightly lit and upright as usual and didn't notice him looking.

Before the session ended, Charlotte gave them each a tiny vial of pills, intended to help with intimacy. "Take one pill thirty minutes before you plan to engage in sex. The chemicals help remove any neurotic dispositions or anxieties that might occur with new partners. We want to encourage a familiarity, a routine, early on. You may experience boredom at first, but that's normal," she emphasized. John nodded but didn't tell Charlotte that they had already broken one of the rules by sleeping together the previous week, after their dinner at So Noodle! They had kissed again outside of the restaurant in the dark and then outside their apartment, and in the hallway and living room, each time more prolonged and feverish, the spontaneity that began with the dinner invitation fuelling a slippery looseness between them. The only mention of CoupleTrue that night had been the small logo on the condom packet.

The lack of sharing with Charlotte was something they both agreed on prior to the session, although John noticed that Rachel had been hesitant, even fearful.

"It's only because I'm generally a very private person," he said, meaning to reassure her. "I don't discuss those things even with my close friends. To me, it's something that should be kept between two people."

"I know, I know," she responded. "I just feel, I don't know, like I'm lying. Shouldn't we be completely open with our therapist?"

"She's not just our therapist," John said. "I'm not sure what to call her . . . but I just feel like there are things that shouldn't be judged or analyzed immediately."

But they were judged anyway. Charlotte said in their session that normal, well-functioning couples should engage in intimacy three times a week, and she guided them toward an app developed by CoupleTrue. In her presence, John had downloaded the app and inserted his date of birth, height, dietary restrictions, and basic lifestyle choices. It physically pained him to be so direct and to see himself reduced to such tiny data.

"No more indecision or uncertainty," Charlotte said, and again John felt a small part of himself react strangely to the locked statement. Was this what he really wanted? Was this what they had all agreed on? In his last relationship, he had struggled with expressing his own needs in relation to what was considered a normal, socially acceptable timeline. It hadn't been a singular event that caused the unraveling of his relationship with his ex, but a series of missed meals, miscommunications, and lack of planning.

Part of his enjoyment of his night with Rachel was that it hadn't been suggested by CoupleTrue—he had just done it, and the ease with which she reciprocated his affection had made him confident. That wasn't something you could parse out verbally or in languages of logic. He liked that he had initiated something that worked just as well as a bullet point activity on a leaflet or a footnote in an email. It was also true that this was something he did at work all the time—finding creative, rebellious solutions to projects that seemed rigid to the point of failure—and he relished those satisfactory moments.

He then found himself horrified at the prospect of treating Rachel like a project. He had, in the past, made it a point to never compromise in relationships—it had to do with his family and how strict they were with him as a child—but now he sincerely wanted this to work.

"What are you thinking about?" Rachel asked.

"Nothing," he said, shaking himself out of it. He took her

hand. "Let's not keep anything from them in the future. I feel bad about that."

"Okay," Rachel said, a little surprised at the turn of events. "Thanks."

Now, outside of the clinic, John shook his vial in the evening's fading primrose light. It was Friday; people were leaving work, umbrellas drawn like huge floating skirts for the incoming rain. The pills were buttery yellow, round, with a hard ridge down the center.

"Well," he said, turning to Rachel. "What do we do with these?"

IT WAS TRUE, THEY became bored almost instantly. The tedium that plagued them was not one of irritation or frustration, but a softer, mellow kind, one that reminded Rachel of lying under her parents' living room fan as a child in the summertime.

"I remember feeling this way before smartphones and the internet," Rachel said. They were now both lying on the sofa, heads apart but feet tangled together. John looked up slowly.

"Yes . . . yes! And it also feels like, it feels like when you're young, and you're sitting in the car in traffic, and you start to fall asleep because it's so warm . . ."

"Right, that too. Also, waiting for the rain to stop because you want to go outside . . ."

They talked a little more, then napped, then woke up again, pouring themselves enormous wobbling glasses of water that created raised liquid islands on the kitchen countertop. Rachel took another pill, John took three. She looked at him.

"Charlotte said it was fine! She said you could take up to six per day."

Somehow, she found this funny, she found him sweet, and she laughed, holding his arm a little. His flesh felt wobbly, and it made her feel wobbly too. "Hey, John," she said suddenly, "can we look at your sketches?"

She could tell that he was nervous at her request. In fact, she had thought about asking him a few times, but the moment never seemed right. She realized John responded better to spontaneity; he tended to work himself into severe anxiety if he had time to stew over things.

She continued: "I just feel like I want to get to know you better, and since it's something you're doing every day, I wondered if you wanted to share. But I'm okay to wait if you're not ready."

To her surprise, he agreed, but immediately became mute as he took out his papers, his books, and showed them to her wordlessly.

"And these are people you know?" she asked, trying to begin a conversation, looking at the various faces and limbs and bodies.

"No . . . well, they're not exactly figurative sketches," he said. "They ambiguate the space between figuration and abstraction."

Rachel tried to understand as she looked down at a sketch. It appeared to be of a man crawling on his hands and knees, the head small, grape-sized, curled under his chest. The man's fingers were elongated, merging with shadows or dirt, she couldn't tell, and his hands were bent too far at the wrist. It was unclear whether the figure was reaching forward or pulling back. *It's not a person,* she suddenly realized, *it's a scene of tension, of not being sure where you want to go, who you are.*

"It's how I felt after my mother moved back to Japan," John clarified. "She lives in Fukuoka now. They wanted me to take over the family business. In metal scrapping."

"Oh," Rachel said.

"But we don't talk anymore."

"Oh."

John began putting his books away. "Maybe I'll paint from this sketch later. It might become part of a series about feeling in between, in between races, in between obligation and desire."

Rachel put a hand on John's shoulder to steady herself. She was burning up from the heat of feeling a certain way toward him, of wanting to embrace the inside of his body. How could she explain it? She was feeling empathy, and she was feeling sorrow, and she was feeling regret. Was it the pills? Or was she falling in love? She was afraid.

She decided that it would be nice to lie down on the living room floor, to ground herself. Taking deep breaths, she looked at the ceiling, the blank space on which the shadows from the television and the computer screen mingled and washed it blue. She thought of John, how he had formed these membranes, these elastic boxes around himself. You could push against them, she realized, you could pull and try to pry one open, and a peek inside would show you that he was a good person. She hoped he saw her that way too. That he would try.

Her thoughts continued to drift. She thought of the space above their apartment, which would be another apartment, and the space below. How each apartment, one after the other, felt just like another in-between space, another semitemporary holding meshed in with the others.

"He had another apartment. Just like this one. For his mistresses," Rachel said.

"Hm?"

"My dad. He would bring me there when he was supposed to be looking after me. I would play in the kitchen. I'd pretend that there was a door in the back that would take me back home, to my mother and my real father. Like I was living in a parallel universe, and I could just go back to the real world, in the space behind that door."

"Your . . ."

"Sorry?"

"You just said your 'real father.' Who is that?"

Rachel realized her mistake. She didn't like speaking of this to anyone, not even Charlotte, who had brought up this question to her several times in the past. To her, the distinction was always changing. It was impossible to differentiate what was real—the truth that was prone to disappearance—and what was unreal, namely, things that were always present but artificial. She had two fathers, but she did not know how to treat either. One was her birth parent; the other raised her. Neither knew her fully. Her mother, at one point, had loved both, and, at another point, had despised both. What was real, what was the unreal? She had asked herself this often as a child when looking at the mirror in her father's old apartment, and occasionally she would see a dark-haired adult woman shifting in the background, a figure that could have been herself in ten years' time. The scent of lemon, the spray her father was careful to use every time. The accents that changed but also remained fixed to one axis, the lie that was a musical note. The adults that drifted in and out of her life as a child—she couldn't remember all their faces, but she remembered the way they moved past her as if she were a cheap lamp in the corner of the room.

"I don't really want to talk about this right now," she almost whispered. She could feel the pill's effect wearing away, leaving her: Goodbye.

As she prepared for bed, she thought she heard faint laughter. *That's odd.* It disappeared. She watched sleepily as John switched off her bedside lamp, plugged in her phone, kissed her good night. But when he left the room, the sound came back: a muffled, muscular laugh, as if someone was playing a game or watching a late-night show in the other room. As she was pulled into sleep, shapes interlocked and burst behind her eyes; she saw shadows, she saw lemons. She saw John. *Don't leave me too*, she said to him as her consciousness zeroed into squares, then dots, then nothing. *Don't leave me.*

LIFE COASTED ON. RACHEL celebrated her thirty-fourth birthday. John went to yet another friend's wedding and found some silver hairs in his beard. Rachel donated some clothing to a thrift store and cut her hair.

CoupleTrue sent more and more red-starred reminders and deliveries of increasingly romantic gestures—cases of red wine and blood-colored roses, vouchers for jewelry shops, recommendations of good tailors and restaurants. John was the main recipient of such reminders. He ignored most and instead surprised Rachel with drawings of gardens and pigeons, tickets to "An Evening with Ishiguro," elaborate home-cooked meals, and reruns of *Downton Abbey* when she had menstrual cramps.

They received a letter. "Your nine-month anniversary is next week," it stated. "Please accept this gift voucher for a couples spa weekend at Highton Moors retreat."

Highton Moors was an hour's drive from where they lived, and the voucher was only valid for one day, the anniversary of their first meeting with Charlotte and their moving into the apartment. Rachel knew it was a busy work period for John, but when he sighed aloud and said, *I really can't afford to stop working right now*, she couldn't help but feel offended. Still, she tried to call CoupleTrue to cancel, but a man told her that the voucher's date simply couldn't be amended and was strictly nontransferable.

When the car came to pick them up, shiny in the purple dawn, they had been in the middle of one of their rare arguments. Rachel knew that John didn't really want to go but that her reasoning—

that CoupleTrue had used their money on this trip, and it shouldn't go to waste—wasn't the full truth. Some part of her was also looking forward to the minivacation, to spending time with John away from their day-to-day lives, although she didn't articulate this. She didn't want to sound needy.

Arriving at the white-walled complex, they were surprised to see several other couples at the entrance, some already robed and drinking tea, others with luggage. Rachel saw that there was another Asian man and woman standing near the counter waiting to check in. They began talking to one another.

They were a very new couple, and they showed these signs outwardly by talking about their therapy sessions. According to the woman, they were a rare, destined match and so had been invited to come to Highton Moors earlier in their relationship. Rachel had not known that there was such a tier. Speaking with them, she tried not to let her irritation show. She hated that their names were Yan and Wing, their voices still glitched with an accent and their bags oversized and ostentatious, stamped with designer logos.

"Rachel, Wing is also from Suzhou," John said. Wing began to speak excitedly to Rachel in dialect, but she shook her head curtly and said, "I'm sorry, I don't speak Chinese." She didn't know how to say *anymore*, so that was always the answer she offered. Wing then laughed. "Ohhh okay, sorry, sorry," and Rachel thought it sounded like he was laughing at her. She excused herself abruptly and indicated to John that she wanted to go to their room immediately.

"What was that about?" John asked when they were out of range. "You were being rude."

"I'm here to relax, not socialize," Rachel said.

"I just thought it would be nice to talk to them. They seemed like a nice couple and you heard Wing, he doesn't know that many people from Suzhou."

Rachel fumed. She felt her anger spreading like an allergic reaction, but she was also afraid of letting go. She knew she had upset John, but still, she couldn't help blaming him. He suggested that they take a break, and he left the room. She started to unpack, and with each item she took out from the suitcase, she thought of another thing that she disliked about John. It was her default method of analyzing someone when she was upset.

John is messy. John likes to stay up late. John jokes too much. John gets too stressed. John doesn't take me seriously. John doesn't love me.

She considered that last one.

My perception is that John doesn't love me.

She asked herself why. She thought of the lack of chocolates and flowers, the way John seemed almost violently avoidant of anything CoupleTrue suggested. A while ago, she had teased him for even signing up for CoupleTrue—knowing him now, she understood how strange and rigid the whole program must have been for him. He had looked at her, confessed that he actually hated it at the beginning.

"But I'm still glad I joined."

"Yeah?"

"I met you, didn't I?"

Taking out the last items in the suitcase—John's toothbrush and hers—she thought of how, in some weird way, she was still happy. At least she was feeling something; at least everything wasn't just a neutral wall of beige. She touched the bristles of his toothbrush against hers. His were long and soft still. Hers were spikier, ground down by repetitive actions of trying to scrub away something stubborn. She liked how different they looked, how they didn't exactly fit together but were still there, pressed up against each other.

THEY MET UP AGAIN at the baths, which were situated at the back of the complex. A CoupleTrue assistant showed them how to properly distribute the Epsom salt into the water and handed them a leaflet titled "Ten Questions to Ask Your Soulmate," which they ignored. The assistant left and mentioned another couple would be joining them shortly, for "bonding." They both entered the water silently.

The bath was Roman style, a large, open marble space with long benches and a tall, white atrium. One wall was entirely a large picture window from which they could see out onto a plain of mossy knolls and bunched wildflowers.

"Something strange is happening," Rachel said quietly.

John turned.

"Something strange is happening," Rachel repeated, and this time she lifted one arm clean out of the water, a slim finger pointing. "There."

A dove-gray mist rolled over a stone wall in the distance. Through it John thought he could see a parade of crawling shapes. He panicked, thought, *They followed us*, and then he saw two figures, people who looked similar to Yan and Wing, slowly wrestling or embracing. Their limbs rolled over the stones, the rocks, their expressions blank and wide-eyed. Then the fog burst, and there was nothing but clear blue air, the sun announcing the afternoon.

"John? Are you all right?"

"What? Oh, yeah. I'm fine."

"Are you sure? Because you were muttering to yourself. What did you see?"

He was about to ask her the same question, but just then someone entered the atrium.

"Look who it is!"

Wing had already made himself comfortable in the bath, placing a soaked hand towel on his forehead. "Yan's on her way too. Wow, it's so romantic here," he said, and Rachel wondered if it was a joke from the way he said it.

"I mean, look at this view—really."

They all looked out the window where just a moment ago a pallid fog had formed. Rachel, noticing that John still seemed disturbed, whispered to him again, "Are you all right? Let's please go if you're not feeling well."

"Hey, John, not so bad, right?" Wing said. "Perfect place to propose. Yan and I are definitely thinking about it." He looked at them expectantly.

Rachel was about to respond, but just then John climbed out of the bath and stalked toward the door. Following him with their towels, she apologized to Wing. "Sorry, actually John has a lot of work to do, enjoy your bath."

In the elevator, she tried talking to John, but he stayed quiet. In the room, he seemed to still be processing something. He suggested that Rachel go on ahead and join the evening's activities—cocktail hour and dinner with CoupleTrue staff and the other couples—while he stayed in the room and worked. They needed time apart, he said.

Hearing this, Rachel regretted her earlier irritation, feeling small and anxious at the thought of extended separation. She turned over a CoupleTrue leaflet in her hand as she weighed John's suggestion. Going to Highton Moors was an almost foolproof method to upgrading your relationship, the testimonials boasted. Many couples conceive their children here. Many couples get engaged or go back home and adopt dogs. On the last page, there was a photograph of a dog.

As Rachel left for dinner, she felt a familiar pang at the sight of John's blue-light glasses sliding down his nose. She felt the desire to push his glasses up and kiss him on the forehead. Instead, she vanished quietly through the door.

THE NEXT DAY ON the car ride back home, both John and Rachel received an email from CoupleTrue asking for feedback on the anniversary trip. *On a scale of one to ten, how would you rate your relationship before visiting Highton Moors? On a scale of one to ten, how would you rate your relationship after?* Both of them read the message passively. Both of them ignored it. Ten minutes later, they received another email, from Charlotte: *We noticed you did not fill in the feedback form. Please do so at your earliest convenience. We need to assess this information in order to upgrade your relationship. Also, I would like to book a session for you both soon.*

John silently moved the email to a special folder in his inbox, where dozens of unanswered emails from Charlotte were archived. He could have just deleted them, but somehow he wanted to keep a record, evidence of the therapist's surveillance over them.

Rachel looked at her calendar for the upcoming weeks, trying to see where she could fit in Charlotte. The tiny squares were filled with appointments, client meetings, happy hour drinks with colleagues, and something more intangible: the presence of John.

"Should we talk?"

John's question made Rachel tense instantly.

"About?"

"Well. About the trip. About us. I guess."

Rachel was silent. She felt a sudden desire swelling in her, the urge to say, *Let's just break up then*, to open the car door and walk out onto the street alone. How many times had her mother done the same to her fathers? How often had she seen one parent reject the other, again and again? She thought about the toothbrushes.

But then John touched her hand.

"I just wanted to say I'm sorry." He turned to face her, peering into her eyes as if seeking some part of herself that had disappeared. "I'm sorry, Rachel," he repeated.

After a while, she said quietly, "I'm sorry too."

John let her cry. When he hugged her, she smelled sweaty, as if she had been asleep for a long time.

"There's nothing wrong with you, or me," John said quietly, so quietly she almost couldn't hear. "The only thing wrong is what people expect of us."

They pulled up to their street.

"Are you tired? How about we go out for dinner? We can go check if our favorite place is open."

They dropped their luggage off. On their way to So Noodle! John paused to look into the community garden. The pigeons had disappeared, but there were a bunch of robins sitting around. One of them pulled at the long grass, snapping it off. The sound was crispier, louder than he expected.

The neighborhood was quiet. Rachel remembered John's earlier comment about the couples inside the apartments being cardboard cutouts.

They were surprised to see that instead of the modish logo for So Noodle! there was blue construction fabric covering the entire front of the restaurant. A large slit revealed itself, flapping in the breeze, and they stepped through it. Inside, the space looked the same, but all the staff had changed—they knew this for a fact, as they went there every other week. Over the past few months, they had become regulars, and the green-haired waiter always served them. It had been their place. John remembered how nervous he had been to kiss her that first time, how he had debated all through the evening about doing it, but she kept saying strange things that surprised him; it took him out of his thoughts, and he realized then that she was very sharp. He loved that most about her, her keen intellectual curiosity, and there were no instructions whatsoever in the app that taught them how to nurture this quality. She was just like that.

"Is Alvin around?" John asked one of the new people walking by. The restaurant was so dimly lit that they appeared as shadows, copies of the figures he saw in his dreams and in his sketches.

"Alvin. Alvin?" they said. "Hey Gary, do we have an Alvin?"

Someone said from the back, "No Alvin here. We're not open yet."

Rachel whispered to him, "The menu's changed too."

He looked. The same items were featured but were even more distilled modifications of foods they had eaten before. In the back, he saw a tall, wiry shape, and he almost called out, *Charlotte?* but then he saw one of the new waitstaff glaring at him, a dishrag hanging off his arm like a wet tongue. The Charlotte-shaped figure disappeared. They left.

Back at the apartment, they looked at their luggage and somehow felt as if they shouldn't unpack. The apartment was motionless, filled with both generic and personal items—there was the chair that had become John's chair, there was the seat by the window where Rachel liked to drink her tea. In the bedroom, some of their clothes hung limply in the closet. Various bottles of collected spices and condiments crammed the kitchen cabinets. There was the door behind the washing machine that made strange noises whenever John loaded the laundry. There was the mirror that sometimes laughed at Rachel as she walked past. And outside: cardboard cutouts of people, shadows, figures like ghosts.

"Do you ever feel like the world just keeps moving on and on and on?" Rachel said. "And we're just struggling to catch up?"

John thought about what she was saying. Boxes in boxes in boxes—he had imagined Rachel as another box, but it turned out she was wrestling to get out too, the same way he was.

"Yeah," he said. "But in some way, I think... I've always felt that. Even when I was young. I never wanted to follow my mother's schedule. I always just wanted to do other things, and I always hated it when I was told I had to go to school or go home or to my grandma's. I just remember this feeling of being dragged everywhere. Now that I think about it, I was kind of miserable."

"I can see that."

"I never told you this, but my ex contacted my mother once. She said it would be better if we all got along, for the marriage. I hadn't even talked to her about marriage yet. I think she just expected that I would go along with her five-year plan."

"What? That's insane."

"Isn't it? So yeah, anyway, I found out, and I think some part of me really hated her after that, the fact that she made me feel like I didn't even have agency over my own relationships. But when I tried to talk to her about it, she made it seem like I was being immature. So . . ."

"Jesus."

"I don't feel that way with you though."

"That's funny, because I *was* that person. I had that five-year plan."

John took Rachel's hand. "Hmm."

"I thought I would be married by now. I remember in my very first session with Charlotte, she told me that I was a perfect candidate for the program. She said all I needed to do was follow their advice exactly."

"Mmm."

"But it didn't work. Over time I cared less and less about marriage, I think. And then I realized, I don't care about any of that stuff, really. It's just what I thought I wanted because I had read about it in books or seen it in films. Or because Charlotte told me that's what I wanted. She was so convincing, you know? And so judgmental whenever I even mentioned that maybe I wanted another form of relationship. And my parents . . ." Rachel trailed off.

They looked at their suitcases. They didn't want to unpack. But they also didn't want to separate.

They were still holding hands.

Later, after they had made their decision, a representative from CoupleTrue arrived at their door. He looked at his checklist again. *John and Rachel—Severe—Noncompliant.* Earlier that day he had received a call from Charlotte at the clinic, and she had informed him of the couple's transgressions. On her list of grievances was John's lack of communication, Rachel's indecisiveness, and their combined disobedience. It had not gone unnoticed that the couple had been absent from most community activities at Highton Moors and were openly ignoring emails, phone calls, rituals, and instructions. CoupleTrue had to take immediate action.

The representative rang the doorbell, but there was no sound from inside. Pressing it again, he pushed his ear up to the door, and he thought he discerned some faint movement, heard some rustling, but still no one came to the door. He looked at his watch.

The doorbell chimed angrily again and again, a blunt noise, an interruption. John and Rachel were not there to answer.

Not in This Neighborhood

Someone had brought edibles, so a sliver of the party stood by the edge of the living room, sloshing their bodies together and gasping over a video. As T walked up on the group, she watched the screen, unmoved, as an oyster-silver dog stood on its hind legs, then sprinted through a set of sun-faded red hoops. Crescents of laughter. She didn't really know anybody at this party. Someone she met through a Facebook group had introduced her to his roommate; that person in turn had invited her out for drinks with his friends, and someone in the group had mentioned Jill. Now it was July 4, and she was at Jill's family house, a white-clad mansion in the suburbs.

That morning she had seen an elderly basset hound ambling on the sidewalk and watched as the owner folded down to scoop up a large, stinking mass of poop. "Good boy!" the woman had said. The hound looked up with its sad, red-rimmed, wet eyes. T noticed that people here talked to animals a lot.

Back where she came from, dogs and cats were wild and lived in forests. People kept cricket fish as pets. One summer, her younger sisters caught eight from a field nearby. T had been studying for exams all those long, hot months, her face constantly angled over books, but occasionally when she needed a break, she would let these tiny critters crawl around her desk before releasing them back into their small round tanks. When they died, her sisters cried, and T couldn't help but feel sad too. She missed their tiny honey whirs; polite, rhythmic, short-lived.

Her mouth was dry. She needed a drink.

The kitchen was new with America: brass faucets, fridge magnets, organic eggs, a silver butter tin, waffle towels in slate and blue. It was quiet and massive, in a way that reminded her of the beginnings of the vintage Earth films her parents would watch late at night. She closed her eyes for a second, letting her vision dart around in the plumbed darkness. With her arms resting on gummy marble slabs, she felt her skin shrink. She recalled the apartment she used to live in, how if she reached out with her fingers anywhere in the space, she could feel the walls that divided her and her neighbors.

"What are you looking for?"

T opened her eyes and caught the stare of another girl standing a few feet away. Embarrassed, she lifted her hand as if to wave, but then said, "Just some water."

The girl—young, wearing a burgundy hoodie with sweatpants—found a plastic red cup somewhere, poured water and ice into it.

"Here you go."

"Thanks," T said. "Are you Jill's sister?"

"Mmm. Hannah."

Hannah couldn't have been older than nineteen. T saw a softness in her face, peach baby hairs. An unusual straightforwardness. Her youth was comforting and clean.

T was more used to teenagers who hid in their bodies shrapnel of hungry black sunlight. She saw it in her home city, when the first curfew laws pushed people out onto the streets, rattling and shouting before being silenced in clouds of tear gas. She heard it on the radio, when young activists were interviewed, and then later, in the silences between dry reports on the weather. She saw it in the shuttle when a woman strapped herself in and began slicing her forearm with her thumbnail, over and over again, until meaty striations appeared. These people had been her colleagues, classmates, neighbors, relatives.

She thought of these people as she drifted through the gathering, motivating herself to initiate conversations. Her new neighbors: the women with wine teeth, the men in sweaters snapping open beers, the people hanging off corners of things high on low-grade weed.

She wore jeans and an ill-fitting t-shirt she had bought at a supermarket last week. At the register, the line had been long with people and trolleys of things red, white, and blue. She looked down at her sad, small metal basket. A carton of eggs, tinned fish, some juice that stained her teeth a florid yellow. She remembered she didn't have anything to wear to this party. When the line bumped forward, she randomly grabbed something near the cashier that looked like her size: a shirt that said, in bold cursive, *ME TIME*.

It had been a bad choice, but it wasn't as if anybody noticed. Early in her arrival she had figured the best way to blend in was to let people talk about themselves. She laughed at respectable intervals, although she knew the laugh was a poor facsimile, a false preservation of the way she used to laugh before she had moved away from home. Everything was an echo. Canned laughter, tinned fish.

On her third or fourth lap around the room, the conversation began to loop and glitch—popular television, food, politics, social media, inane gossip about mutual acquaintances, politicians who made food, television about social media, the politics of gossip—and she strained herself trying to keep up, smiling and frowning and laughing. Some people wore sunglasses, even indoors, even as the sun was setting in its cold, yolky way, so that she couldn't see their eyes. Seeing herself reflected in those pale, hard, mirrored ovals, she felt even more alien, and she was reminded of the photographs and fingerprints the U.S. border control took of her three months ago. In a windowless room, separated from everyone else on the shuttle, they had made her sign a form that listed the political conditions back home, how she was arriving not as a tourist or a licensed professional but an extraterrestrial refugee.

Leaving the airport that day, she noticed how clear the sky was compared to home. A small car followed her all the way to her motel, but after that nobody attempted to contact her. For a while she sat in that motel room alone, paranoid, ordering takeout and paying delivery people in soft, weathered bills left outside the door. A few weeks later, she moved into an apartment complex in an area she had chosen one day on a map, not far from New York. She called no one; wrote to no one about the news. She realized she hadn't spoken more than a few words aloud since she landed.

Back home, people spoke far too much, but their voices were empty—their *how are yous* and *nice weather today* and *good luck on your exams* rattled around hollow, the emotion that once stood behind them long gone. In some ways, the patterns of the party mimicked these interactions. A few times she mentioned her home planet, and people murmured a few words of sympathy, but then Molly needed another drink, and Gabe suddenly remembered a funny joke he had heard at work, which made Penny take out her phone, and Jill absolutely needed to show people photographs from her latest ski trip.

Swapping one form of isolation for another, she convinced herself she had made the right choice, but it made the party no less strange, no less surreal as she watched from a distance the slow-moving crowds crawl through bowls of snacks, drinking and playing cards. She remembered at school, years ago, an economics teacher telling her about these people. "Earth is our neighbor planet, so we share many of the same characteristics, but they are especially known for their love of entertainment," he had said. *Bread and circuses*. Games and beer. As if there was nothing else in the universe they could be doing.

T HAD FOUND HER apartment through Jill's family friend, a woman named Barbara who had gotten her real estate license after her third divorce. She encouraged T to do the same.

"I set my own working hours, I get to meet great people, and honestly, it's so much fun," she had said as she walked T over to the complex. "I don't actually manage apartments. I mainly do family houses, but Jill said you needed help, so I found this great spot for you." Barbara winked, her eye shriveled and caked in blue powder.

"Now, remind me how I pronounce your name again?"

T said her name. Barbara tried to repeat the sloping vowels, but she fell flat on the tones and twisted off the end with a sour twang. T shook her head, smiling, repeated her name, but still Barbara laughed and said it wrong, flapped her hands and said, "I'll just call you T, honey, that okay?"

The apartment faced a river, which frothed and soaped against the edges of the rough banks. T heard animals there in the early violet mornings, frightening sounds she had never heard before: branches cleaving themselves from trees, skinny-necked ivory birds skimming the air, things ripping and dying in the woods. The place was bucolic, tamped down with a sort of stunned, blinded friendliness that was distinctly of this world. Older couples and single women inhabited the other apartments. Directly across from T lived a woman named Marta whose apartment faced the road. When T first moved in, Marta had crept out into the hallway and made a strange comment about how young T seemed, what a nice view she had. "I would have liked that apartment myself, but there's a long waiting list apparently," she said.

T saw Marta next when she took out the trash. Marta was

standing in the hallway, anxiously wiping away the rain from her coat, creating a damp painting of moisture on the carpeted floors. She explained that she had been locked out, how her daughter lived nearby and would arrive with an extra set of keys within the hour. She kept talking, emphasizing how cold she was. Then T realized she wanted to be invited in.

"Oh, thank you, you're an angel," Marta said, taking off her coat but not her shoes. "Oh, it's so strange. My apartment is just like this, except . . ." She ran a hand over the wallpaper. "In reverse."

T wanted to be a good host, but she was tired. Earlier that day she had been interviewed at the bank for her new account. It had been almost a month, and she still hadn't received approval. She felt vulnerable, invisible, without something that connected her to these institutional structures. If she had an account, she thought, she could find a job. If she could find a job, she could earn money to buy food, save up. If she saved up, she could leave this place and move to a better apartment. If she could move to a better apartment, she might be happier. If she was happier, everything would be fine.

"Do you have children? Of course not, you're so young. I had Mary when I was nineteen. Can you believe it? I was a baby. Kids these days are waiting until their thirties, and I think that's the way I should have done it. Nineteen and I don't understand my daughter now, not at all. She says she never wants kids herself, so there goes my chance to be a grandmother. Do you have any water, by the way? Oh, I'm so sorry to barge in on you like this, it's just that I saw something on the news and then decided to take a walk."

T poured a glass of water and brought it to her tiny round table, where Marta had already sat down and made herself comfortable. T thought, *She has very long arms.*

"Did you see the news? A woman killed herself and her daughter, and she did it somewhere in the neighborhood . . . I figured out the address and I walked over there. I just had to take a look, the woman was a single mother . . . her daughter was only nine years old . . . so I took a few pictures of the house, only to post on my Facebook . . . you know, something like this has never happened before, not in this neighborhood . . ."

Marta finished her story but showed no indication of leaving. Tapping on her smartphone, she showed T her Facebook account, scrolling through to the newest post, for which she had written a three-paragraph text explaining the circumstances, the history of the house, and how the story would inevitably impact real estate value in the area. *My daughter lives very close by,* she wrote, *and I have been settled in the area for over fifty years now. Something like this has never happened before. I hate to think of how this tragic incident will affect the community I know and love.* Under her post, there were already twenty or so comments, likes, and sad-face emojis. *Heartbreaking, such tragic news,* one of the comments read. *It looks like a beautiful house. My grandmother lived in Fairlake for twenty years.* Another said, *Thanks for this. The state of news media and journalism has been in the shitter lately. Keep up the civilian reporting. We must take care of each other.*

Of course T knew about the murder-suicide. The woman and child had been from her planet.

She kept the news on constantly throughout the day as a reminder of how quickly things could change. At first, the reports had been neutral, even kind toward foreigners. *Earth welcomes asylum seekers. Refugee visas to include up to 1.7 billion people.* But then people like T actually started showing up. Some of them were dead within weeks, unable to manage the transition. There were so many of them, and not enough space, not enough jobs. The narrative changed from a language of community to one of singularity, of hostility. *Earth rejects visa expansion for extraterrestrial youths. Deadline for exodus looms. Another extraterrestrial body found in the river. Riot breaks out at factory as extraterrestrial workers protest discrimination.* Late at night, drinking wine and taking pills, T found online videos of pseudointellectuals espousing conspiracies on space propaganda, mutated genes, and phrenological analyses alongside lectures by flat earth theorists and montages exposing politicians as reptiloids. Here she realized that mistrust was embedded deep into the human psyche.

After that evening's intrusion, T avoided Marta in the hallways, watching through a peephole to see if her scrunched figure was nearby. She allowed the distance between them to grow long, full of unfamiliarity and polite, forced gestures when they saw each other on the street, in the same aisle of the supermarket. Occasionally, she would receive a Facebook friend suggestion for Marta via an algorithm: *People you may know.* Every time, she pressed *Remove*. She wondered if this was what it was like to be neighborly.

AT THE PARTY, SOMEONE asked about how her former home had managed a contaminated water crisis, and she explained that the government had implemented a system that citizens dutifully followed, and not many people had gotten sick in the end.

"That's one of the main benefits of an authoritarian regime, right? Not like out here in the Wild West."

"Yes, that's true," she responded, smiling weakly. She did not tell the woman that there had been many people who had stayed within the lines, who had read all their contracts before signing anything, and still had found themselves in compromising positions. She did not say how on their phones there had been tracking devices, tiny drones blinking overhead. She did not tell the woman how if someone even thought about breaking the rules, there would be a neighbor calling a hotline, turning them in. She did not mention how her parents had suffered in their final years from chronic anxiety and depression before succumbing to a cancer that everyone in their generation seemed to be sick with.

She excused herself to the bathroom but had trouble finding it. Jill, walking past, saw her, pulled her to one side—"Hey, you can use my parent's bathroom upstairs"—and soon T was in an almost-silent part of the house, the sounds of people drinking and partying like a distant laugh track. Jill and Hannah's parents, T noted as she peed and looked at the monogrammed face towels, were Bill and Eleanor.

The bathroom was at once opulent and chaotic. Sturdy spined books rested on a ledge, fringed by dainty embroidered curtains. She saw *The Life-Changing Magic of Tidying Up* next to a group of reading glasses, tangled together with their bead lanyards. A tiny glass sculpture of a Boston terrier stood in a carved-out space behind the toilet. The sink was a gigantic ceramic marvel with hot and cold taps, and when T washed her hands she splashed the water around a little to demonstrate just how much space she had. Another whole person could stand beside her, and they would still not be touching. She recalled the sensation of her body being pressed in a crowd, pressed onto an unyielding floor, and she shook that feeling away as she reentered the party.

She ate some hot dogs and drank a cup of warm, flat beer to appear ceremonial. She could try to pretend, she could adapt; she could be that friendly neighbor. But she was still unsure of the social rules. She spoke too early or too late in conversations, and as the night went on she became less alert, less perky. She had studied enough human body language to know that people didn't enjoy talking with her, that they felt weighed down by her presence. She looked around for anyone else who might be like her. But the problem was that everyone here looked the same as they did back home.

All along, these people on Earth had assumed there had been

other places to go, other planets to start anew on. Her arrival had shattered that illusion. Everywhere was just the same, from the soil down to the languages. The verisimilitude made them uneasy. Her body was a reminder: No matter how far you travelled, there were always things you couldn't escape.

ONCE, HER FAMILY HAD visited Earth, back before everything had changed. Her father, a scientist, had been invited to a conference.

"When is it?" T's mother had asked. "The twins can't take any time off school. Exams are coming up."

Fortunately, the conference was scheduled for December. They bought overpriced new winter clothes, which T's mother was anxious over—*Surely it would be cheaper there* and *Will they even let us go outside?*—and looked up photographs of snow. Nobody told them that it never snowed in Las Vegas.

Before they left, T's father had told them that their trip had to be kept a secret since not many people knew that the borders had opened to interplanetary travel recently.

"They probably won't let us leave the resort grounds," he had told them. "And no talking to strangers."

At their hotel, the concierge looked up their booking while their father tried to get a signal on his small handheld radio.

"The connection here is poor," he remarked but then was distracted by the presentation of two giant, gold cards.

"This is your room key," the concierge said. "Breakfast is from nine to eleven. We have twenty-four-hour room service also. Please enjoy your stay."

"Two keys . . ." T's mother said. "Could we have an extra one? For my daughters?"

The concierge looked at T, nineteen at the time, then to her twin sisters, ten years old, smartly dressed, sharp-edged like two brains wired to a single computer. He clacked on his keyboard, and then T had it in her hand: freedom, at least within the confines of the resort.

"You're in charge of your sisters," her mother said, pulling her close. "Don't leave the hotel."

For three days they ran around the faux-marble fountains, the indoor palm trees, the men in suits. They stuck their faces on smoked-glass windows, ogling at the cars and sunlight and people walking around. They ate glazed donuts and played chess.

"The food is weird," one of T's sisters said on the fourth day, at one of the resort's lavish, gold-frosted restaurants, poking at plates of fried potato and meat. "I miss our food."

"Don't complain," T said, and was about to say more, but her eye caught a pale, unshaven man sitting by himself not far from their table. He was looking at them, and there was something uneasy in his directionless posture, the way he sat and ate as if he had nowhere to go. She noticed immediately that he was distinct to other people in the room—he dressed differently, for one, in a long gray coat and a white-streaked baseball cap. Everyone else was wearing colorful, silky indoor clothes, as if they had just arrived from their rooms. T then remembered it was December on Earth: cold.

The man had a strange bruise on his chin, a flowering growth of purple. He was drinking a coffee, or some kind of dark liquid. He sipped at it hurriedly, like a rabbit running over a patch of grass. Then T saw him ask a waitress for the check—it was so elegant, the way he pinched his fingers and made a W with them—and in the same motion, very fluidly and quickly, he wrapped a fork and a knife in his cloth napkin and slipped them into his pocket.

When their server came with the bill, T told him what she had seen.

"Maybe you can catch him before he leaves," she said.

After they left the restaurant and were back in their rooms, one of T's sisters asked why she had talked to the waiter.

"The man stole."

"Just a fork and knife?"

"It's wrong."

The other sister chimed in: "I think the man needed a bigger meal. He looked poor. He looked sick."

All day after that, T felt terrible. She kept thinking about the man's outfit, and whether he was really poor or sick. How he moved like a block of gray sky, like something you did your best to ignore as you went on with your life. She wondered if they had caught him, if he knew that she had told. She kept waiting for him to turn up, like a bad dream, but they never saw him again. Soon they were leaving.

On the weeklong shuttle trip back home, T heard her mother crying late at night.

"I really thought we would see snow," T's mother whispered. "I feel so silly. Even the girls didn't care that much."

Her mother softly cried some more, and T heard her father say, "We'll go back another time, okay? Maybe when the twins are older. Another holiday."

She thought about this now, alone at the party. When it came to choosing where she would migrate to, she had chosen America simply because she didn't know any other place. In catalogues, the photographs were spectacular: red, rusty canyons, parks and trees. But she should have known better, should have known that the man with the bruise in the café would tell her all she needed to know about Earth and its distractions.

Now her parents were long gone, and her sisters were living different lives. One of them had become an activist and protested space colonization and poverty tourism; the other was a lawyer. They hadn't kept in touch all that much, a message here and there. T suspected they didn't even know she had left. Both of them had stayed.

Who was right, who was wrong? At night, T turned over the choices in her mind like a coin, feeling herself slip and morph into her dark dreams. In the mornings, the grayness of her curtains, her floor, matched how she felt as she poured another cup of coffee, took another lukewarm shower, set up her sticky computer to spend another few hours looking for jobs. It had been so long since she felt the rightness of anything. In America, people liked to call it *gut feeling*, as if there was something in your bowels that could provide spiritual clarity.

She had read in a research paper about how immigrants gained new microbiomes in the first few months of arrival to the U.S., their bodies adapting quickly to new foods, new fats, and sugars. Scientists also noted a loss in gut diversity; in some cases, people lost the microbiomes they had inherited at birth from their families, making them more vulnerable to disease and infection. But her gut was silent, soft, yielding. It told her nothing, except that she was always hungry.

HANNAH OFFERED TO DRIVE T home since everyone else was too high or drunk to figure out which car was theirs. When T refused, saying it was an inconvenience, Hannah shrugged and said it wasn't a problem: She was a night owl anyway, and she had just been reading in her bedroom.

On the way over, T asked Hannah questions about herself, in the way that she felt adults should with younger people. She learned that Hannah was a freshman at a prestigious college that her parents couldn't exactly afford, but she had received generous funding. She was a history major.

T's apartment wasn't too far from Jill and Hannah's house—which made them neighbors too, technically—but she was grateful for the ride. She had forgotten how utterly dark it was here, how it felt like the thick velvet night was moving against you, blotting out vision. As the car pulled up to the end of her block, a strobe light flashed on somewhere, and T thought she must look so washed out, so dry and small. She wondered if Marta was home yet, if anyone was in the apartment building at all, or if they were all out celebrating with their own friends and families.

"Can I ask you a question?" Hannah said.

"Sure."

"Can I ask you what living there was like? I don't know anything about it."

T looked at the young girl next to her.

"You really don't know anything?"

"I don't. I know that it used to be different. That's all."

T thought about a message she had received from a close friend just before she left.

Did you see one of your neighbors has been arrested? the friend said. *Did you know them?*

After a long while, T had texted back, *Maybe. I don't really remember them.*

Be careful. I heard from someone that the police have a list of people they're targeting.

T thought of the hollow of her building's staircase at night when she took out the trash. The Earth immigration letter she received, how it felt like a hallucination, and even in the days and hours leading up to the shuttle's departure she couldn't fully convince herself that she was leaving, leaving it all behind. But she did not think of the policeman who had knocked on her door, the *yes–no* questions he had asked, the names he made her write on a piece of paper before he said she was free to go. She tried not to remember how her friends treated other traitors. She just carried around the same feeling she had when she was nineteen—watching the man steal, knowing everything around them was festering from the inside out anyway.

In the obsidian night outside, there were animals hiding in the trees, veiling themselves from predators, eating others. On her home planet, there were cars that patrolled the streets, thickets of men in uniform lining the walls of train stations, apartment buildings. There were things she had done that seemed to be of another person's life, like the way one might look at photographs of their mother and father as teenagers, recognizing the origin of something that was already a phantom. But she wasn't there anymore. She was here, and this young person was looking at her, waiting for an answer.

"Maybe another time," T said. "Thanks for the ride."

She got out and felt the warm air hit her tongue, her skin, a blank touch. Everything that had once thrilled her about this place—pictures of first snow, the highway lanes of supermarkets and pharmacies, the weedless suburbs—felt like a memory of a memory of itself, a videotape wiped over.

Outside, simple colors chartered the skies, pulling heads of smoke from their hazy, bright constellations. Sparklers ran across the lawns, and T knew there were hands attached to them, but because of the darkness, it looked as if they were floating circles and spikes, sputtering fast into oblivion. When one firework ended, another began somewhere else, and she imagined the entire neighborhood lighting up like one of those old telephone switchboards, the exchange of laughter and air and sweat like lines in the grid.

In that lit-up darkness she imagined herself calling her mother, just as she used to when she was in school and her parents were still alive, her father calling out, *Can someone get the phone?* and her younger sisters playing games over too-loud music, a party every night. *Yes, my darling, what is it? I'm making dinner*, her mother would say, and she'd tell her, *I'm coming home this weekend—see you soon*, and in the background, she would hear one sister scream, *You're cheating!* and the other huff angrily. Her mother would say, *What—I can't hear—be quiet! What did you say?* and the line, only a few kilometers' distance between them, would spit and fizz, threatening to drop out on them, on this memory. *Hold on*, she would say, *hold on. I'm coming home, Ma. Wait for me.*

Acknowledgments

The following stories were previously published:

"Mycomorphosis," *The Rumpus*, Aug. 29, 2022

"Please, Get Out and Dance," © 2021, Ysabelle Cheung, as first published by *The Margins*, the digital magazine of the Asian American Writers' Workshop

"Patchwork Dolls," *Granta*, Aug. 18, 2022

"Galatea," *Slate*, Oct. 29, 2022

"Herbs," *Joyland*, Dec. 8, 2022

Gratitude:

To Yanyi, for a year of mentorship, and your lessons of self-care and survival.

To Kaitlin Chan and Karen Cheung, eternal members of the Marmo Fan Club, for your keen eyes, friendship, and Lactaid.

To my readers, who generously gifted me their time and patience: Eunice Tsang, Özge Ersoy, Jacqueline Leung, Siqi Liu, Mimi Wong, Tochukwu Okafor, Ophelia Lai, Brady Ng, David Walter, Meg Charlton, Jessica Kingdon, Peter Molesworth, Ben Bertaccini, Alex Elias, Vicky Woo, Larissa Abaidoo, Ned Carter Miles, Susan Blumberg Kason, and Marshall Moore.

To Bleak House Books, which inspired "The Reader," and Jia Tolentino, whose essay "The Age of Instagram Face" inspired "Patchwork Dolls." To *Joyland*, *Slate*, *The Rumpus*, *Asian American Writer's Workshop*, and *Granta*, who published earlier versions of the stories inside this book.

To my agent, Jade Wong-Baxter, who believed in these stories. To Robin Miura, Lynn York, and the team at Blair, who published them.

To Willem, for encouraging me to begin again.

And finally, to the teacher who said I would never learn to read; the magazine publisher who made me doubt my own words; the men who followed me home from school; and the authoritarian figures who dictate what we can, and cannot, write and say. You gave me a reason to write these stories.